TRANSFERENCE

TRANSFERENCE

BOOK ONE OF THE NARRATOR CYCLE

IAN PATTERSON

Book Cover & Illustration by Barış Şehri: https://baris.editionstilemizon.com/

Editing by Melinda Crouchley: https://www.melindacrouchley.com/

Paperback ISBN: 979-8-9909170-0-2

eBook ISBN: 979-8-9909170-1-9

— First published edition, 2024 —

To my wife, for always encouraging me, and to my daughter, for being the catalyst I needed to start.

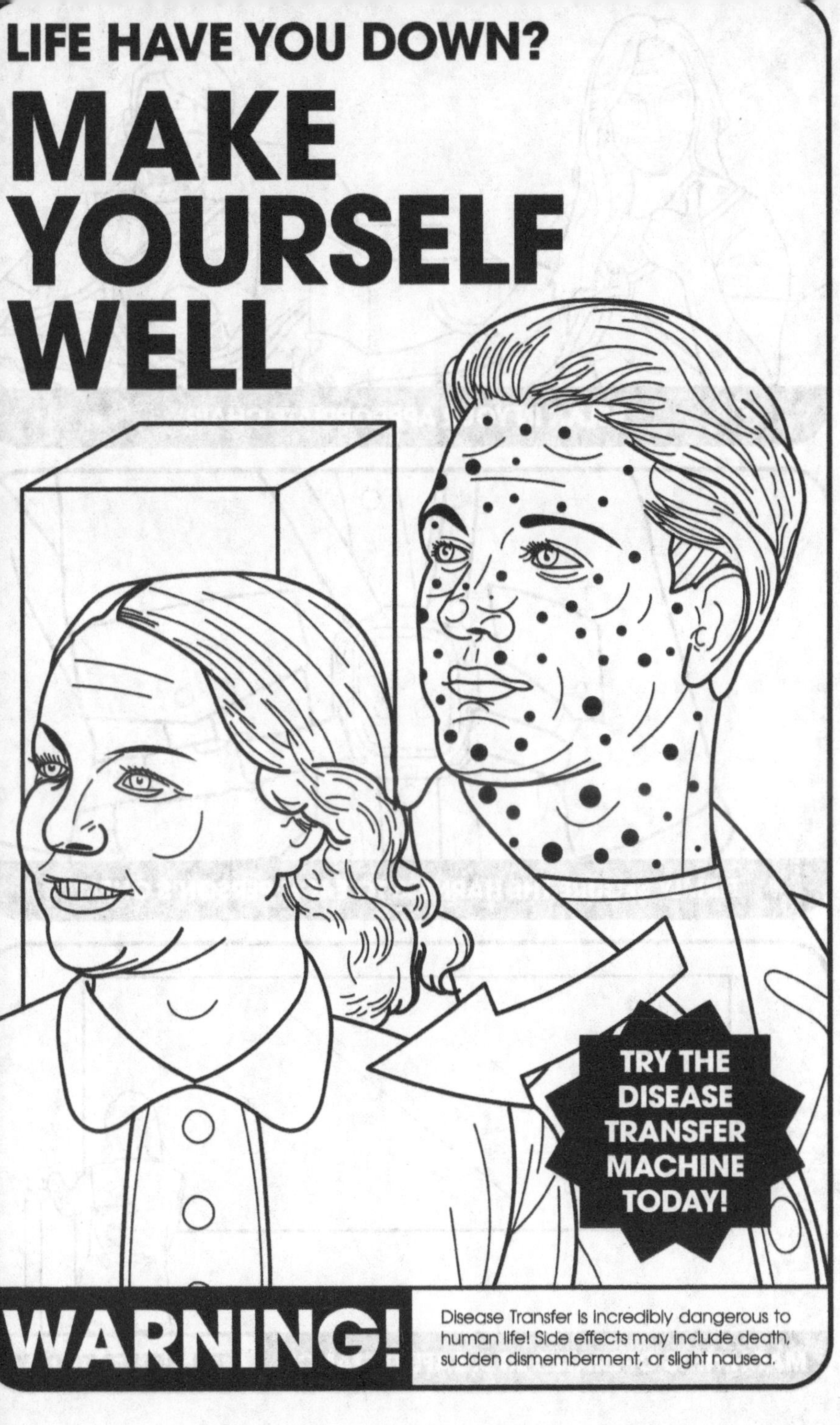

LIFE HAVE YOU DOWN?
MAKE YOURSELF WELL
TRY THE DISEASE TRANSFER MACHINE TODAY!
WARNING!
Disease Transfer is incredibly dangerous to human life! Side effects may include death, sudden dismemberment, or slight nausea.

RELAX IN YOUR APPROPRIATE CHAIR

FIRMLY SECURE THE HARNESS TO EACH PERSON'S CHEST

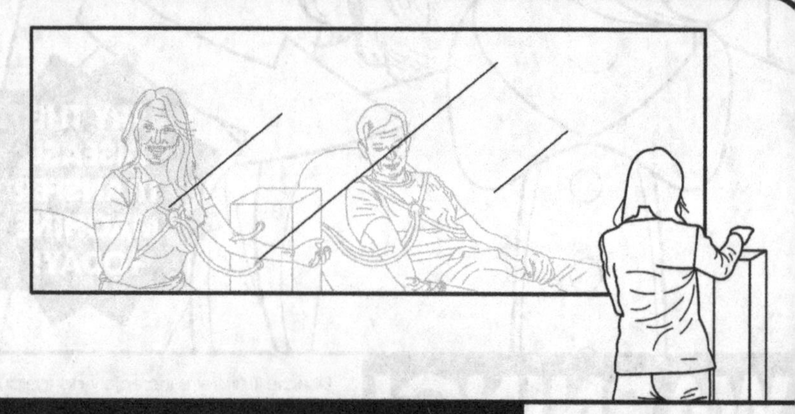

MACHINE IS OPERATED AT A SAFE DISTANCE
FEEL BETTER TODAY!

"He who fights with monsters might take care lest he thereby become a monster. And if you gaze for long into an abyss, the abyss gazes also into you."

Friedrich Nietzsche

Chapter 1

From darkness, I emerge. The world is shining, impossibly bright. I clamp my eyes to shut it out. Discomfort bleeds in no matter how hard I close them. *I itch and ache all over.* A pile of thin blankets covers me. They're a white so pure it hurts to look at. *I have to move. I have to stand. I'll die if I don't.*

Like a newborn again, I take my feeble first steps, testing the strength of my legs. I've lost coordination, certainly lost muscle. I shake my head, thick with drugs and sleep. *How long have I been out?* I make it to the door before some small nuisance tugs at my arm, and I tug back. Thin wires fall out of a machine on the far side of the room, and a mild beeping fills my head. *Is that just in my head?* I look around the room, bracing myself on the cool metal door frame to stay upright.

Some sort of hospital. It's cramped and smells of disinfectant. Not the nice kind either, the kind they use when they think you're not waking up. It's full of white and silver machines that whir and blink and spin and pulse, *and they're screaming in my skull, and it's too much I can't fucking take it.*

I squeeze my eyes shut as nausea washes over me and threatens to take my legs. My heart thrums in my ears. I grip on to the door frame with the meager hand strength I have left. I breathe in deeply, hold it, and then exhale. Eventually, my heart rate drops back down, and the nausea settles.

Thoughts force their way into my brain like needles into a formless wad of yarn. *Someone will know that I'm awake, someone will come. They'll have information, and I'll pay them and then leave.*

At the thought of payment, I panic. If you live long enough on the edge, the terror of an unknown bill can make you spiral. Adrenaline shoots through me, bringing with it some much needed clarity, and I flip my left wrist and navigate the screen installed there until it displays my credit balance.

I can feel my eyes bulging as my legs go weak again and threaten to collapse under me. *How big of a job had this been? Holy shit, how much did I gamble?* It's more money than I've ever seen. *Breathe, just breathe.*

The door to my room swings open behind me, and I lock eyes with someone who looks familiar. He's tall, wearing a white lab coat with a short graying beard, and has a very stern look on his face. He's handsome, in a grizzled, fatherly way. His face tugs at my memory, but nothing surfaces from those murky depths.

He breaks my gaze, and shaking his head, sighs. "Sit down before you give yourself a heart attack too, Nicholas." He motions back to the bed. I mechanically make my way to it, and sit.

Taking a stool across from me, the man adjusts his lab coat and then continues. "Here's the story, you took a big one, a real fucking nasty one, and I was pretty certain you weren't coming back. Now I expect that you've got some short term amnesia so I'll fill in some blanks. Stop me if it starts coming back so we can talk about more interesting things.

"Your name is Nicholas, my name is Brian. We've known each other for a decade, we're friends, but some days I really wish we weren't. You're a *Sicko*." The name stirs something in me. "That means you make a living trading money for taking on other people's diseases. It's a fucking stupid existence if you ask me, but you hire me to look after you and keep you alive, and I get a cut of your earnings."

With a sudden anger, he grabs my wrist and flips it over and taps his pointer finger against my screen. "Did you see how much coin is on this thing? That's after you paid me too, I wanted payment before the procedure because your odds were pretty bad. Now that's enough to quit, so stop fucking doing this. I am tired of piecing you back together." He accentuates each of these last words with a finger thump on my wrist, and after a long pause he says, "I don't want to see you die on my gurney." He looks away.

Scattered memories start to flood back in. A handshake in a dark room with someone smoking, sitting in a sterile room with my body plugged into a disease transfer machine, Brian yelling at junior staff and shaking some images, a machine showing erratic vitals, and then absolute darkness.

"How long have I been out?" I ask, slowly. Talking is difficult. My tongue feels alien, too thick, too rigid. I have to concentrate on each word. They come out heavy and wrong, like my mouth is full of cotton.

"Three months in a medically induced coma, one month of treatment before that. At first, you were heavily drugged to keep the pain levels low. And when—" He makes a small choking noise, and then continues after a pause. "And when we knew you probably wouldn't make it we had to put you under so your body could focus on healing."

I'm stunned. My eyes find the mirror behind Brian and it's painfully clear what the time has taken from me. There are bones visible through my hollow, pale skin. My already angular face is sunken now, outlining my high cheekbones, sharp nose, and narrowed green eyes. My head is bald except for a few long straggles of black hair. I don't remember being an attractive person. Now I'm terrifying. Shaking, I ask in a small voice, "What the hell did I take on?"

"Cancer, a particularly nasty lung cancer. The bastard you traded with lied. I fucking told you he would, but you saw the money and went for it anyways. Stage one he said. Hah! No, it was fully metastasized. He showed you old scans, hired fake doctors to convince you. He probably figured you'd die, because that's what Sickos do. You bite off something too big and it takes you out, and those rich, smug fucks get to keep on living lavishly."

"Can I report him to anyone? That kind of shit's got to be illegal–"

Brian interrupts me. "What, did you lose your brain while you were under? Illegal?! No one gives a shit what those cats do. You report him and the best you could hope is that the

Inquisitors ignore you, otherwise you might wind up in a gutter at the bottom of the Boroughs. Just be happy you woke up from this one, that's the only thing you're going to win today."

Brian stands up and walks towards the door, but something gnaws at him. He pauses and turns back. "Look, kid, you're going to be fine. Your cancer markers are back to baseline, and somehow you even woke up from your coma. I'd say it was a miracle if I believed in anything like that. Now, you're going to rest in this bed, I'm going to send down some really shitty hospital food, and you're going to eat it all and think about what you're going to do with your time now that money's not tight. And you better not tell me you're going to take on another job, or I'll kick your skinny ass."

"Do you mind bringing the food back yourself? I might have some more questions by then." Memories have started to come back, images through a haze of smoke, and I know a lot rides on what moves I make next.

Brian rolls his eyes, turns, and shuts the door behind him without responding. Smiling, I lay back down and close my eyes. *I like Brian, he's a good sort.*

The Disease Transfer Machine, or the Box as we call it down here, was invented some time before the city. It's always existed here, the primary thing shaping our lives. It sounds noble at first, *the elimination of disease*, until you realize it only works that way if you can afford it. For those of us in the lower levels, it's the thing killing us. It's the only job we can find. It's the poison that we can't stop eating.

Do I know how it works? Not a fucking clue. One person sits on each side of the giant metal box, various tubes extend from it and connect to each of them. There's a giver's seat and a receiver's seat, and no one else in the room when they turn the thing on. It's a strangely intimate thing, sitting across the room from your destroyer. There's a feeling of great suction all over your body, and then the misery sets in. The symptoms start like a bucket of ice water dumped on your shoulders. I've always wondered what a great relief it must feel like on the other side.

The backbone of our economy is built on it. The very rich trade their diseases to the very poor for *appropriate compensation* agreed on by both parties. But realistically, when you're poor enough you're too constrained to know what appropriate compensation is. Some people have tried to create laws around it, establishing contractual requirements and base pay for different diseases. They don't mean much though, there was always someone willing to go under the base pay, there was always someone that needed the money badly enough to take the risk. Laws just give the illusion that what's happening is fair. Of course, it's not.

This new caste of people, the perpetually ill, were *lovingly* nicknamed Sickos. The working poor hated them for the ease they got their money, the middle class decried the horrors of rampant capitalism they represented, and everyone tried to buy their services when their own bill came due.

I know some that only take on petty viruses. The money's shit, but it's consistent and it won't kill you. Most people start small though, and then slowly work their way to the more serious stuff as they get older. We've all got plans drawn up for who gets the money when we kick it, and everyone just hopes they can set their family up to get out of this existence. But almost no one does. Sometimes, very rarely, someone would gamble big and win, and the promise of that kept everyone else trudging on.

I was sick of seeing it. Watching families get torn apart after someone took on that one, big job and lost. Watching the money from it run out. It was never enough to sustain those left behind. And then watching the youngest of them start down the same path, perpetuating this never-ending cycle of shit and death. Most of us didn't live past 35, less than a quarter of what the wealthy elite live.

When I was 10, I watched my father waste away from a cancer he took to set up our family. In the Boroughs we're taught to honor the sacrifice of our family. *They die to give us a better life.* Fuck that. When he finally passed after months of pain I didn't feel pride in his death, I just missed his presence. Glorifying his death felt cheap. He didn't sacrifice himself so I could live, this world ate him up until there was nothing left, and then tried to feed me some hero's tale. I refused to eat that bullshit.

I knew two things then. The first was that I wasn't going to bring a family into this meat grinder. The second was that if I was going to sacrifice myself, it was going to be to put an end to it all, not to continue the cycle. My father's death made it clear to me—it has to stop, someone has to stop it.

I knew it would be rare though. The cost of transfer goes up exponentially as a disease progresses, and finding someone willing gets less likely as the survival chances dip. There's still a market when life expectancy is discussed in months or days, but there are only a few people ready to make that sacrifice. People like my father. Still, it can take precious time to negotiate after that, and not all deals close in time. I needed to find someone willing to pay almost anything, but with a disease I might actually survive from.

I met my chance in a smoke filled bar. He told me about his early diagnosis, about the positive outcomes that were expected. All the while he smoked rollers from an ornate, silver case. But I saw the flash of rust red that he buried in a napkin after a coughing fit. And I saw the lie behind his eyes every time he said, *Stage 1*. I stared at the burning tip he held between yellowed fingers and imagined the flame growing to consume me. Then I told the man what he was going to pay me.

A few hours pass before Brian shows back up, the promised tray of hospital food in his left hand. They print the whole thing in the mess hall upstairs out of nutrient blocks. It turns the tasteless cubes into something resembling meat and vegetables, but they still all taste vaguely similar. I've had some time to think, but in that instant all I can remember is that I'm a living thing that's been starved for four months. Brian hands me the tray, and I attack the slab of nutrient meat without stopping to grab cutlery. Somewhere in my brain I know it's terrible, the same old shit I always eat, but at that moment I've never tasted something so wonderful. At least it looks like real food.

"Slow down, you're going to make yourself sick! Shit, if I knew I was feeding an animal I would have just thrown raw blocks at you." Brian's voice sounds rough, but he's smiling while watching me eat.

I pause, set down the food, and wipe my hands clean on a napkin. I motion to the stool opposite me and he sits down. I break off the printed knife and fork from the side of the tray and cut off small, measured bites. We don't talk while I eat, and when I've cleaned the plate I set it to the side and look into his eyes.

"Brian, thank you. I knew this was going to be a terrible risk going into it, and a lesser friend would have abandoned me while I was comatose. You're a good man, and a better friend than I deserve for sticking this out."

He nods, waiting pensively for what is coming next.

"I've got to ask for help again though—" Anger rises in his face so I put up my hand to pacify him. "Not with another job, I'm done with that. Look, I went into this taking the biggest risk of my life, and knowing damn well that I'd either die or get a chance to make a difference. And thanks to you, I get that chance. Now what comes next may not be to your liking, but this is why I took on that cancer. I had a plan going into this. You can't stop me, I need you to understand that. But I'm going to give you the option, do you want to know and help me willingly, or do you want me to tell you what I need and leave out the why?"

"I don't know what the hell you're talking about, so let's just start with what it is you think you need," Brian says, gruffly. Smart man, there's enough bullshit in this world that it's good to not entangle yourself.

"Tell everyone I died here, including your staff. Fake the reports, take one of those stiffs out of the morgue, say it's me, and burn it. Then get me out of here without anyone seeing."

He stares at me blankly, an endless stream of questions formulating behind his eyes.

"Look I gave you the option here, that's what I need, and if you want to know why, I'll tell you. But if I tell you, you're involved. And you know what that means. I'm heading down a road, and it would be great to have a friend with me, but I won't take that risk for you."

Brian opens his mouth, and then shuts it several times. His glasses have slid down the bridge of his nose, and absent mindedly he pushes them back up. Resolve builds behind his eyes, and when he speaks next I already know that he's in.

"Fine, Nick. I'll bite. Why do you think you want me to fake your death? What're you planning that you need to be dead to do?"

I breathe in, I've been prepping these next words for the past few hours, feeling their flavor on my tongue. I lean forward on the edge of my bed and stare into his eyes. "I'm going to tear the system down, the whole disease transfer system. All the remote units work with guidance from some central processing station in Sun Gate, and I'm going to cut the cord. I'm talking about maximum possible destruction, scorched earth, nothing standing afterwards. Maybe they'll rebuild it, or maybe they don't even know how to anymore, but it will give us the time we need to break out of this cycle. I'm going to take the fight to those fuckers, make them pay for what they've done to us. I'm going to burn it all down."

Brian erupts in laughter. He throws his head back and roars, and when he's done there are tears streaming down his face. I was prepared for anger, but not this, and my face sours. "I'm afraid to say you've lost the plot, Nick. You're one man, and you can barely walk right now you're so weak! You're going to infiltrate Sun Gate and tear down the system. Fuck, that's rich. So tell me, Nick, how in the hell do you plan to pull that off?"

I flip my left wrist out and show him my screen. I show him my credit balance, and his eyes widen in terror. It's a sum that even breaks his concept of reality. "Brian, I knew the cancer had metastasized. I knew it, and I made that fucker pay for it. I knew it would set me up to change things. People don't take jobs like that unless they're ready to die and leave the money for their kids. Finding someone is rare, and he didn't have the time. So I took the gamble. I bet on you—"

Anger flushing his face, Brian stands suddenly and slaps me across the face. I reel from it, my body is too weak for abuse, and for a moment I go limp across the bed. My head pounds. Slowly, I sit back up, and seeing what the blow did to me, Brian sits back down. He's still furious, but he won't hit me again.

"Trust me, I know I deserved that," I say. "It's a small con-solation, but in the event I died the money was all going to an account that you had access to. I figured you'd have some ideas on how to improve people's lives with it. But I lived, and it's a long road from here. So you wanted to know how I'm going to pull it off? I'm going to do it like the rich do it, with excess funding, and all the fancy toys."

Brian stares at the floor, his arms resting on his knees and his back hunched. It takes me a moment, but I realize that he's crying. I think about putting my hand on his shoulder, but remembering his slap from moments before, I think better of it.

He looks up eventually, and wipes the tears from his face. "You're a real asshole, kid. You know that?" There's love in his eyes, and pain. It hurts me worse than the slap ever could have. "I want you to just choose a boring life, get fat and be lazy, drink too much and have some kids. Shit, you've suffered enough to earn a bit of enjoyment. But people like you, well I should have known you'd only choose more suffering. I don't know what it is you think you have to prove, or who you're trying to convince that you're worth a damn. I'll help you. You've already proven that you'll be dead if I don't. I guess I've always been a sucker too, I've spent too much time around your lot. If this is really what you're planning, I'll be beside you to see where it leads."

Chapter 2

Rain pummels me, and I embrace it. *So this is what being reborn feels like.* I'm wet all over and getting colder by the minute. But I also haven't felt this good since I started being a Sicko, and I let it soak in. *I just had to die to get here.* Through the closed door behind me, Brian is putting my plan into action. My life as Nicholas Fiveboroughs is ending back there through official reports, a solid cover story, and the charred remains of someone that no one remembers.

Here in the city, your name is nearly as good as your retina scan. Our names were crafted by the city. All the people in my family were named either Nicholas or Nicholette, and we came from Five Boroughs, the slum that ringed the outside of the metropolis. This naming was supposed to give some order, we were the only family with that unique name combination, but it's just another way they keep us in our place. No matter what had happened in my life, no matter how far I'd risen, I'd always have been a Fiveboroughs.

If I kept that name, it wouldn't be long until the city tracked down my mum. She was the only one from my family still living, if you could call it that. My da's stomach cancer paid well. My mum still lived on that money for the most part. She kept the house in order and took on seasonal colds to make the money last longer. I would not have her pay for the crimes I was planning.

Realizing that I've been sitting still for too long, I lower my head against the rain and start moving. I move quickly up the street, starting the long climb to one of the richer districts. If I was going to stay anonymous, if I had any hope of infiltrating Sun Gate, I needed a new face.

The city is built like a circular, three-peaked mountain that's separated into five distinct zones. It's completely enclosed, but you'd never know it. The walls create a constant video stream that's meant to resemble a day and night cycle. The colors even change with seasons and reflect the city's internal weather. It gives an aura of spaciousness, like when you walk into a room lined with mirrors. Living here, I never think about the walls. There's just the city.

Ringing the city at the bottom is the Five Boroughs district. It might have been separate places at one point, but no one cared enough to continue to recognize them. It's mostly full of Sickos, the working poor, and those slowly marching toward starvation. The only thing further down the hill from us is the sewers that recycle our waste and water, and the smell of it pervades everything in the Boroughs. We all mostly look out for each other down here. Everyone's been laid low or missed a meal, so we share when there's a surplus.

Up the hill is Meadow Hearth. It rings the city up to the base of the three peaks and is by far the most diverse region of the city. Every corner is alive with some hustle at all hours of the day. The red light district occupies a quarter of it, and the rest is full of small cafes, bars, shops, hospitals, and street vendors. It's a place full of honest people, mostly, who just want to work hard and get paid decent. It's also where the rich come down for their wild nights and fancy brunches. Brian's hospital, where I've spent too many nights getting patched back together, is there.

From here, the city splits into three peaks of high rises, sky scrapers, and megatowers. The lowest of these is Sky's Reach. There you'll find working-class elites and high-end services, the type of things that only the rich can afford. The buildings are tall and purposeful, and although they're well constructed, they're not lavish. That's where I'm heading tonight, and it's the highest I've ever made it.

Past Sky's Reach, guards patrol the streets to make sure the riff-raff doesn't climb too high. The second tallest peak is Cloud Spire. It sparkles over the city in fantastic silver and glass that seems to glisten even without the sun. From what I've heard, it's mostly full of new money. People living lavishly, loudly, and with little concern for resources. Partying is a way of life up there, and those from the Boroughs that claim to have seen it first hand tell stories of great costume balls with food wasting on tables and rivers of wine flowing into cups.

Beyond that is Sun Gate. The massive golden tower at the center of the city extends up into the sky and looms over everything else. Up there is wealth and power I can't even comprehend. It's a mystery to everyone, I've heard even those in Cloud Spire can't get access. It's all political elites, old money, and enough Inquisitors to wage a war up there. The servers for the Disease Transfer Machines are somewhere in that golden tower too. I always start to feel vertigo if I look up at it for too long.

I bring my eyes back down and continue climbing.

"You can't just waltz in here and expect me to clear my schedule! I have clients, they're important people, they make appointments with me because I'm damn good at what I do, and they do not accept it if I cancel them!" Michelangelo is gesturing grandly and spilling his rose colored wine on the pristine, white tile floor of his studio's rear lobby, the one he only tells *certain* clients about, as he yells at me. I absorb it calmly and smile back. Then, as if seeing me for the first time he adds, "Also, I must say Nicholas you look terrible, darling. Is this the best work that doctor of yours can do?"

"Shove off it, Micah. I know you don't work on Tuesdays or I wouldn't have stopped by. Besides, it's called a favor for a reason, and you know damn well that you owe one." Not many know Micah's real name. He would certainly prefer that I didn't, and it immediately makes him blanch.

Micah Skysreach, or Michelangelo as he's known to his clients, is a beauty of a man. Anyone in his profession has to be. Of course, you really can't tell how much is natural and where his handiwork starts. He stands a head taller than me, and his muscular frame dwarfs my shrunken form. His face is angled and chiseled, and his dirty blonde hair hangs in a ponytail behind his head. Micah also has certain *proclivities* in the red light district that have left him with several cases of syphilis, an embarrassing affliction for someone in his position. Over the years, I've helped him cure them and keep it quiet, and he found the discretion very valuable.

"Yeah, alright, fine. You got me. There's nothing on tonight's schedule, but I was really *enjoying* some wine." At this, he motions to the adjoining doorway, and I understand that one of his guests is likely upfront *enjoying* the wine with him.

"Sorry to interrupt you, but it's urgent. Please send whoever is up front home, and I'll pick up the cost. I need your best work, I need it tonight, and I come with cash to make sure it's worth your time."

Micah raises his eyebrows and smiles. He wasn't expecting this. "Okay, well, I'm intrigued! Let's continue our discussion in a moment. I'll go send my friend along."

He departs, leaving me in the studio. I realize now that my coat has been dripping dirty water all over his floor since I came in, and I put the jacket on his auto-drying coat rack by the door. I'm considering if it would be appropriate for me to clean his floor when he bursts back in.

"Alright, Nicholas, you have my undivided attention. Tell me about this project that you just *must* have done tonight," he purrs at me, sitting on an antique wooden desk in the middle of the studio.

"First order of business—Nicholas is dead, so burn that name and burn that I was here. I need a new face and a new identity. I need it to be traceable, I'm planning on taking on this person's life. I don't care who it is, only that they're reasonably high up and also reasonably unimportant. And before you tell me you don't do this kind of work…well, let's just skip the dance alright? I know you do it, you know you do it, let's proceed from there."

With each sentence, Micah's smile is growing, until at the end he looks fit to burst out laughing. He claps his hands together in excitement. "Oh dear, this is going to be fun! I'll assume that you've come into some resources then, but you probably don't want the most expensive option that I can offer. Before we continue, you know face melting isn't very fun, right?"

DNA assisted skin manipulation, or face melting as it's commonly referred to, is a very trendy body modification for the richest of the rich. There are a few people in the city that are gifted at it, but Micah is the best. And while it is totally legal to alter your body to whatever beauty standard you want, it is incredibly illegal to alter your body to look like someone else. Which is why this is Micah's back-door only business. Through means that are opaque to me, he procures bodies of recently deceased elites who are also not yet known to be dead, and offers them as new skins for those looking to make a societal advancement. Very few people can afford the service, and while only Micah knows the real numbers, I'm guessing it doesn't take very many people to be worth his time.

I laugh and nod. "This is going to hurt like hell I'm sure. What's available that will make a good match?"

"Well if you really want someone rich *and* unimportant—" He looks at me to verify and I nod, so he continues, "then I think we might take a look at a certain young heir that was found drowned in a hot tub last week. Natural causes I assure you," he says while waving his hands grandly.

If I was certain of one thing, it was *not* natural causes. I also don't think Micah was out there killing people for his side business, that would be a step too risky. Maybe the kid had a bad habit of sticking Luna up his nose, who knows.

"It's strange, it never works out *this* well. You must be lucky, darling. Or maybe someone's looking out for you." He winks at me, and then turns around on the desk. He pulls a key from his pocket and undoes a drawer on the backside. After some rifling, he spins back around with a forest green folder in his hand that he extends to me. "Here we go, review this while I start to measure you. Let's see how much work we have ahead of us."

I take it, the front is blank, and so I flip to the first page. Allen Cloudspire greets me, he looks smiling and affable. Being a Cloudspire, his family will be immensely wealthy, but not as connected and important as a Sungate family. He was 25, like me, but the years look like they were much kinder to him. He's handsome, with a strong jaw, sharp blue eyes, and long brown hair that hangs in loose curls, but not so handsome as to stand out from a crowd. If I were to close my eyes and imagine someone that looked rich, his face might pop up as a template. He was perfect.

As I was reading, Micah flitted around me with a tape measure. Occasionally interrupting me to grab an arm, or foist my chin up, to take some obscure measurement. The data was connected to some holographic image of me that was being constructed in the corner. It clarified with each new measurement.

I thumb to the next page in the dossier and find an outline of connections. Not married, parents are still alive, no siblings to deal with, and a couple friends to be aware of. No job—thankfully most of these rich kids didn't work or I'd have to learn a new skill—and no real time commitments at all it seemed. One long term relationship, now ex, that's still somewhat in the picture. There's a section in the folio dedicated to her that I flip to and it immediately makes me crack into a devilish grin.

She's a Sungate and a neoprog. I bet I can use that as a way in. I'll have to resurrect their relationship, looks like she left him recently for Luna use and lack of a political interest. So I just have to be clean and give a damn, pretty low bar here, is that all these rich girls need?

Her photo is disarmingly beautiful, deeply intelligent eyes stare out at me from the page, challenging my assumptions. I keep reading, and my jaw drops. *Dorian (father) and Dorothy (daughter) Sungate are a powerful family with connections to the Medical Authority. Shit, she's perfect, I just need to use her as a way in!* I'm being drawn in by her eyes and luxuriously thick lips, they're brewing a curious anticipation in my guts. Swallowing hard, I flip to the next page and a hard drive falls into my hand. Pulling it out between two fingers I raise it up to Micah, questioning him with my eyebrows.

"Oh dear, that's your *homework*! You see, I only make you *look* like someone, you have to do the work to *become* that person. That little treasure trove is a digitization of his core memories. Sometimes they're a bit fractal with users, but his seemed well established still. After the surgery, I'll install that, but it's up to you to integrate it. It can be a bit, hmmm, overwhelming. It's no small job to distill those after they've gone cold, but that's why I'm the best at what I do, darling." Pride oozes from him, like a cat that's brought home a kill. I nod and tuck it back into the folder.

"I think you're right Micah, this is a perfect fit," I say, motioning with the folder. "Now, how bad is the damage?" I point to a now complete hologram of me. With a few clicks on the screen on his forearm, I watch as my transparent form is splayed open, and then the form of Allen Cloudspire is grafted on top of it. Calculations whir across the hologram, showing differences in measurements all over our bodies.

"Unfortunately for you, dear, this is going to be a very, very painful experience," Micah responds.

Micah hums steadily as he works, I can hear it as I drift in and out of consciousness. The anesthetic bot is a few generations old, and every time I wake up I can hear it click to life and meter out more to put me back down. I don't mind though, I can't feel anything and it makes me aware of the steady progress. Or maybe, aware isn't the right word.

I numbly blink into existence as Micah's humming fills my brain. I fly along behind the melody for some time, alive with the twists and turns of tune, before realizing that there is a tugging sensation at some very distant thing. Numbly, I connect that this tugging belongs to a group of sensations that belong under the header *body*, and in the same moment I remember that I am not just a floating consciousness.

With great focus, I narrow it down to my left leg, and in response my eyes open and I see a great amount of activity in the mirror above my bed. Small robots fly around Micah and latch onto me like giant mosquitoes. He directs them like a great conductor. I buckle under the strain of existence, and the increasing anesthetic, and disappear for some time. When I reappear, Micah is working on my face and our eyes meet.

Oh no dear, that just won't do, his mouth says to my ears, and he manually adjusts a dial on the anesthetic bot. I plunge back into darkness and stay there.

When I wake again, it's as if no time has passed. My eyes open, and I stare up into a grand room that's very different from my surgery site. I'm alone on a bed that seems double my size, and infinitely soft. The hand carved, wooden frame extends above me and white gossamer curtains billow down. A bamboo ceiling fan stirs the air above, and I watch the transparent sheets dance in it. The bed and fan are certainly antiques from the pre-city era, and I've never seen their equal. When I try to move my head to observe the rest of the room, I realize that my entire body is unresponsive, and panic wells in me.

Micah's head appears in my vision, smiling down at me.

"Well good morning, gorgeous. No, don't try to talk quite yet," he says, placing a finger delicately over my lips. "You went through quite an ordeal last night, and there are nerve blocks in place through most of your body. When they wear off you're going to be in a world of pain, so as soon as your fingers move I'll start administering some pain meds. This is going to be a journey. I have you set up in my private apartment so you can recover in peace."

Reaching behind him, he grabs the hard drive from the folder and shows it to me. "Let me be the first to welcome you into your new existence, Allen Cloudspire. Now since you've got all this time on your hands, why don't you start on some of this homework?" He touches the hard drive to my screen, and the files start to transfer.

The depth of them shocks me, these fully formed memories from a different life. New neural pathways arc through my brain, new connections establish, and a myriad of images spill across my eyes. They all feel like scenes that I know intimately, so dear to me to be obvious, but I'm only just remembering them for the first time. It's overwhelming, and I get lost in this sea of who I was before, and who I am now. My hands grasp at whatever they can find, all my muscles are tensing under the strain.

Micah leans in, and injects something into my neck. I relax instantly, but the memories continue unbroken. And I drift through them.

The next weeks are distilled pain. My skin hurts, my muscles ache, my bones groan all over my body, and no amount of medication takes it away entirely. I'd writhe from it—all I want to do is crawl out of my skin and stop existing—but all my limbs are held down to the bed in what look like giant metal sleeves. Every hour, flashes of light emit from them and needles inject things into my appendages. These are bone growth accelerators, I've heard of them but I've never seen one. Electricity occasionally courses through all my muscles causing them to cramp in repeat succession, and pain to lance through my body. All my requests for a mirror have been denied.

Micah visits me frequently, to check on my pain levels and mental state. He sponges down my body to keep it clean, and replaces my catheter and colostomy bags. Whatever human decency I had has been stripped away. Beyond his visits, I am left only with Allen Cloudspire. Always, Allen.

In my moments of coherence, I visit his memories and make mental notes of his affectations, and the acute nature of his relationships. In the moments when the pain is unbearable, I focus on his life as it plays behind my eyelids. I breathe him in. In my sleep the new memories continue, tracing and retracing new neural pathways. It's suffocating and oppressive. The non-stop barrage is torture, and by the second week I have started to lose the boundary between the Nicholas who was and the Allen who is.

When Micah comes in next I tell him, tears streaming down my face.

"I'm losing myself in this, Micah. It's swallowing me whole and no matter what I do I can't stop it. It just keeps going mercilessly."

He pauses in checking my vitals and puts a hand gently on my shoulder. "That's the point, Allen." He only calls me Allen now and it makes me want to fucking scream. "You have to fully absorb this new identity, you need to become this person. You have to be able to understand all of the nuances of their relationships, and react instantly just like they would. In the best outcome, you forget who you were before, apart from them."

Through gritted teeth I tell him, "I can't fully lose myself. I have work to do. I need to keep one foot in the grave so I remember why the hell I did all this."

His grip tightens on my shoulder. "Then keep your memory in focus, too. Let them mix. As much as we're making you Allen right now, we're also recreating him in you. Let him exist with you, not separate from you. Your success depends entirely on how stubborn you are. Thankfully, in my experience that's not a trait you're lacking in any way." At this, he takes his hand back and leaves the room.

And so I focus on the work. As I unpack each new memory, I build a bridge between Nicholas and Allen. I imagine myself explaining to Allen my why, my own histories, just as he shows me his. Two lines of memory course through me, and I realize that I had been fighting to keep them separate, to keep the boundary firm. I let them mix and bleed together. I see myself standing in the background of his memories, a silent observer, and I open the door to let him stand in mine. We stir, and become something new together.

At the end of two weeks, I'm allowed to leave the bed and explore my surroundings. My bones have tenuously reformed, and from here on loading them will help them to grow even faster. The pain, once sharp and present, has receded to a dull roar.

The room I'm in is infinitely more interesting than what I could see in bed. Pre-city era antiques line various shelves around the room, some of them I can only guess at the function. Mechanical toys with huge wind-up pieces are sat next to palm-sized timepieces that spring open at the press of a button. Each is meticulously maintained and free of dust, museum quality I'd estimate. I move from shelf to shelf in awe.

A memory stirs of my father taking me to an antique gallery when I was younger. I walked the aisles of bizarre objects held in glass cases with my hands clasped behind my back. The smell and age of it brought a silent peace to the place. It's only when I see my father load his pipe in my memory that I realize it came from Allen's life.

Micah comes in as I'm staring at some giant metal contraption with letters and numbers on levers. "Ahhh, I see you appreciate my gallery. That's called a *typewriter*, it was used to draft written words back in the day. Still operational too, although the ink has long since dried." I cautiously press down on some of the letters, and watch a smoothly oiled mechanical lever bring up the adjoining letter.

I see a beautiful engraved disc next to the machine and pick it up. It looks like a timepiece, but it's lighter and flatter. I press the latch, and a mirror springs open in my hands. Seeing my face, an animal fear hits me in the chest, and I scream. I shut my eyes against the image, but it's seared in my brain. *It's wrong, that's not me, how can that be me?* I drop the mirror, and it shatters on the ground as I back away and stumble over to the bed behind me. I fall down onto it, holding my head and crying.

Kicking the shattered pieces, Micah says, "Damn, I thought I had grabbed all the mirrors. It's really much too early for you to be seeing them, my apologies." He sits down next to me on the bed, and puts a comforting hand on my shoulder. "Look, most people go into this process thinking that they're taking over someone else's identity, but it's around this point that they start to realize they were in error. We're resurrecting the dead here and bringing them back to life inside you. They're taking you over and it's difficult to maintain a concept of self through it."

He pauses and looks into the distance for some time before continuing. "I'm going to tell you an open secret, most of the society knows this already, but they try to not acknowledge it. How do you think I've maintained my body without aging for so long? Do you know how long it's been? Five generations that I know of, maybe longer before that."

This breaks through to me, and I stop crying. I roll over and sit up to look him in the face.

"Five generations, that's a long time. Longer than face melting can maintain a young form. You see, Micah Skysreach is an idea, and when that idea gets too old, it finds someone from a younger generation to carry the torch. The original Micah died 450 years ago, but each generation adds to his memories and they're all transferred to the newest member." At this, he turns back to look into my eyes. "You see friend, I've been through this before. I don't even remember my old name at this point, and it's better that way. It's hard for you now, but in time you'll adjust. You will be okay."

I'm gaping at him, at the thought of a single being continuing in this way for five generations. It breaks my concept of reality. "How have you not been caught? Don't the authorities care?" It's the only thing I can think to ask.

At this he erupts in laughter, a twinkle coming back to his eye. "Oh they're well aware, trust me. But as long as I maintain such wealthy patronage, they don't dare move against me. And society will always lust for someone that can make them younger and more beautiful."

He stands, and smoothes the wrinkles out of his pants. "Feel free to explore my house, and make sure to rest. I have a *feeling* you won't get much of it once you leave here." He turns and flashes a brilliant smile, and it's infectious, so I smile back. He's a beautiful man, and I can see now in the painful depths of his eyes what that beauty has cost him. He leaves the room and leaves me with my thoughts.

CHAPTER 3

My new body is strong and lithe. I haven't felt such vigorous health before, and it roars in me now like a furnace. In my old life, I spent the majority of my time sick, or recovering, and constantly without enough food. I was rail thin and crumpled from the constant burden, an old man at 25. Now I'm standing in front of a mirror, flexing different muscles that I don't even know the name of. I watch their lines ripple across me as I move, and it feels like power.

My face continues to confound me. At times it's a beautiful mask that I can't take off, and at others it looks like the face I remember, the one I've always had. My chin is strong and proud, my high cheekbones are outlined not from hunger, but from a dominating facial structure. Thick, brown eyebrows jut outwards over my same green eyes, replacing them would have taken too much time. Naturally curled brown hair hangs down to my chin. I keep it loosely bunched behind my head, just like

Allen did. I feel somewhat like an imposter, but after so many hours of learning this person, also like someone I recognize.

I'm a head taller than I was, with longer limbs to match, and the change to my proprioception has made walking difficult, and hand eye coordination laughable. I fell so many times in my first two days from tripping on my own feet that Micah was scared I'd break one of my still knitting bones. So I spend my waking moments training it with the help of a simulation robot. It floats in front of me, a small spherical thing that projects holographic discs randomly through the air that I have to touch with either my hands or feet. It shrieks in annoyance if I don't hit them quickly enough.

I'm terrible at first, and Micah takes to plugging his ears as the constant shrill alarm from the drone echoes through the hallways of his home. But I improve rapidly as I unlock Allen's movement patterns in my memory. I practice timing, precision, and speed drills until I can complete the hardest difficulty. I practice until movement feels second nature again.

Once my bones are stronger, I move on to a combat training drone. Micah tells me his model is very outdated, but that's fine. The drone stands at my height, a mechanized human shaped thing that's stronger than it's thin limbs have any reason to be. We spar in a gym with padded floors, and at Micah's behest I wear protective gear to not bruise my new body. I've never had a need to know how to brawl, I've never had the physique or energy to back it up anyways, and a few weeks spent training won't change that. I just want the basics, in case I need them where I'm going.

We start with the drone teaching me some simple grapple holds, and how to handle charging assailants. It has a thin, metallic voice that constantly points out the error in my form. Every mistake I make is rewarded with a slam to the padded floor, and by the end of the first day I've gone down so many times that I'm glad to have worn the armor Micah gave me. Otherwise, I'd likely be back to bed rest. The drone teaches me a few handy moves to disarm, and a few to incapacitate. But mostly it makes me unafraid to use my body to protect myself, or to cause pain. For the first time in my life, I see that I can be the cause of violence. There's an alarming attraction to it.

I contact Brian discreetly later that week. My screen has been changed to Allen's credentials, but I don't want to give too much away in the message. *Come see me at Michelangelo's, old friend*, I write and hope he will understand. My time at Micah's is coming to an end, and I need to see him before I disappear into a very different society. I need this connection back to who I was like I need water. Without it I feel like I'll disappear. We arrange for him to slip in off the street at night, so as to avoid notice. He comes in with his portable medical bag, unsure of what I'll need when he gets here and prepared for anything. When he walks in my room, I grin boyishly at him.

"Excuse me, I'm looking for some—" He locks eyes with me, drops his bag, and stumbles backwards against the doorframe behind him.

I stand and cross the room quickly, putting out my hand to steady him. I pull an antique chair from the desk in the corner, and help him sit down.

"Shit, kid. I knew the plan and everything, but this. It's so much. I can't. Who is this even?"

"Allen Cloudspire, puffed to make your acquaintance," I respond, mockingly bowing to him. "I do hope you'll forgive the cloak and dagger to get you here, secrecy is of the utmost, good sir."

He doesn't smile. "Look, you didn't kill this kid, right? I'm supposedly a doctor, even if I mostly have to treat idiots that make themselves sick these days. I'm not about to start embracing murder."

Seeing the seriousness on his face, I drop the affectation. "No, that's not my style and you know it. Micah has a closet full of stiffs that kicked it, mostly just from enjoying life too much I think." At this, I tap my nostril. The drug Luna has clawed its way into most rungs of society, and Brian's damn familiar with the toll it takes.

Brian nods in understanding. "Well, speaking of stiffs, I wanted to see if you recognized one while I was here. Because he's surely dead at this point. As I was going through the hospital video record and scrubbing your exit from it, I found something very strange. It turns out your *miraculous survival* had a more understandable cause." He flips through items on his screen until landing on a surveillance video, and I swivel around to get a view.

I watch in silence as a man walks down the hospital hallway and goes straight to my room. It's after hours, and he doesn't even bother with a disguise. He's dressed in a tuxedo and top hat, and looks completely out of place. The camera's too grainy to make out his face, but it's clear enough that I can tell that he's ancient. In the next shot I see him positioning me in front of the Box, but on the giving side. The camera doesn't show the other side, but when the Box turns on I gasp.

"What the fuck? That old man came in and took my cancer?"

"It sure seems that way. I've never seen anything like this. I mean even if someone wanted to do that, those doors are all locked. No clue how he got through them. You know him?" Brian asks, turning off the screen on his arm as the video starts to loop.

"No idea who that is, or why they'd want to save me." I'm baffled. *Why would anyone do that?* There's something here I'm not understanding. My skin crawls with nervous anxiety.

"Figured so, all the same I wanted to let you know about your mysterious benefactor."

"Who almost certainly died so I didn't have to."

Brian nods, and stares at a spot on the floor in front of him, unable to meet my gaze. I can tell the reminder of my death, Nicholas's death, weighs on him.

I pull up a chair opposite him and sit down. "Look, Brian, I need you to understand why I'm doing this. I need you to understand, because without you I'm going to lose my connection back to who I was. If I have any hope of changing things, I need top level access to the society. I need no one to question my presence until my work is done."

He nods again, but keeps his gaze down. I know there's something chewing at him. So I ask the question that's been eating me all these weeks. "Did you break the news to my mum?"

Brian starts to cry, and puts his hands over his face. Through the tears he says, "Yeah I did, kid. I did that because you asked me to do that and it was fucking terrible. I transferred her the money you asked me to, and told her you died from that cancer. Your mom, that poor woman has struggled for so long. You were the last thing keeping her moving, and I don't know how she's going to manage. She just sat there, staring at the wall, and cried. Didn't say a fucking word the whole time."

Like a knife in the chest, the news takes my breath away. *You had to do this, if you didn't the ruse wouldn't be complete. You knew the cost of it, you have to be dead to everyone. This will hurt her, I just hope it doesn't sink her for good. It's worth it, it has to be.*

I focus on this to stop myself from crying, too. "Brian, you have to look out for her. Please, friend, in a month or two maybe it will be safe to tell her the truth. Just make sure she makes it that long."

He stares at me now, unsmiling but with love in his eyes. "There's something cold in you, kid, something this society took and broke when you were too young to stop it. It's in you, just like I know it's in me too. And I see it in your mum too, just like I see it in all the people of the Boroughs. I know it's anger, and it's hate, and I know this all has to happen. There's a fucking reckoning that's been building for centuries and the gate has to burst. But don't let it swallow the people you love. They're the reason you're doing all this."

Tears have started to blur my vision, and I wipe them clear. I put my hand on his shoulder. "I know it friend, I know it."

"So then, what's next from here?" he asks, changing the subject as he wipes his eyes as well.

There's a small noise from the hallway outside, and my gaze floats over to the door. "Micah, you can come in. Don't just sit there listening at the door."

Impishly, Micah strolls into the room with a huge grin and sits on the antique desk next to us. "Sorry boys, I couldn't help but feel a little left out, so figured I'd give a listen."

"You've already got enough on me to put me under if you wanted Micah, and I need more people I can count on. I think you're one of those people, did I get that right?" I ask.

"I don't kiss and tell, gorgeous." Micah winks at me.

"I'm trying to bring down the disease transfer architecture. I want to destroy the servers that they get all their reference data from and cripple the whole network. I've heard from several sources that they're in Sun Gate—"

Micah interrupts me, his eyes wild. "They're not just in Sun Gate, they're at the top of that bloody golden spire under heavy guard and behind a lot of locked doors! Have you seen the Centurion guard before? They're massive brutes that have been melted and brainwashed to hone their killing art. They'll tear you apart, literally. Piss off, I wouldn't have wasted such a good body on you if I knew you were just planning on getting yourself killed."

I hold up my hand. "Good sir, do you take me for a ponce? I'm not a fool boy charging off to fight windmills, I'm a damned Cloudspire, and anything worth doing is worth doing *politically*." I let Allen breathe through me, and it gets both their attention. "A few well placed friends make the longest lever I find, and I've always loved making friends."

I flash them my best rich heir smile, and then I sink back from the role. "Now that I have access to high society, I need to build a network. Allen already has a notable connection in Sun Gate, bloody hell, his ex is Dorothy Sungate, daughter of—"

"I know who she's the daughter of, pup, I don't need the society lesson. And it's *ex* for a reason, if you paid attention to those memories. She's exceedingly cunning, and if she helps you there's probably an ulterior motive. You're playing with fire, tying yourself to that one," Micah sighs.

"Still, she's a good place to start. She has favorable politics, and I bet if I show her that I'm not the Allen she remembers then she'll come back to me. Then I can try to use her connection to get entry to the Medical Authority. It'll take work but it's the best damn chance I have. I also need to find access to a very discreet *gear* salesman, I won't stay out of danger this whole time I'm sure. Do either of you know someone that's hustling on the side?"

Now it's Brian's turn to sigh. "Yes, but you can't trust the man to stay quiet. He supplies the Plague Doctors, really nasty shit, and the bastard's got a loose tongue as soon as drinks are involved. He loves getting ripped and bragging to anyone that will listen about who he supplies. I've heard he frequents half the bars in Meadow Hearth. Honestly shocking that the authorities haven't bagged him, but I guess the Doctors are more of a nuisance than a threat to the rich. I wouldn't get involved with him unless you absolutely have to."

I wince. I want nothing to do with those psychopaths. The Plague Doctors are a militant group that has slid from protest towards terrorism over time. Used to be the worst they did was property destruction, burning someone's house down in Sky's Reach or blowing up a Box, but more recently they'd hired a chemist. Everyone has heard stories of gas attacks in the streets of Cloud Spire, but I don't know how credible they are. The Doctors are no revolutionaries though. They seemed to be more interested in chaos and pain than meaningful change.

"Okay, we'll save that trick for much later then. Micah, I've been wondering about this, how do you intend to get me back to my new family without raising any suspicions? What's my backstory?"

There's a twinkle in Micah's eye as he responds. "Honey, there is no backstory! You came by Michelangelo's to get some work done, and stayed to recover. The truth always sounds the most natural, and no one polite will ask you what work you had done. Besides, you've got those lovely green eyes now, I'm sure they'll just fawn over them when you return."

I knew my time was coming to a close, but hadn't realized how quickly it could end. I swallow down my anxiety. "So, I'll just walk right in there?"

Micah chuckles. "No dear, your days walking are over. We'll call your family tram when you're ready."

I stand up, and so do they. I extend my hand to Brian, and he swats it away and wraps me in a bear hug. My frame is so much bigger than he's used to that he laughs as he hugs me, and I hug the old man back.

He pulls back but holds onto my shoulders. "It's good to see you so alive, kid. Keep it that way. Go up into your new playground and make some friends, but don't forget where the hell you came from. We're all still down in the dirt suffering. You know where to find me if you need me—" He moves back and bows to me. "*Monsieur* Cloudspire."

I chuckle at him. "Thank you, my friend. Micah, we'll call the tram tomorrow."

CHAPTER 4

Anxiety writhes within me. Until now, I've hidden in the shelter of my friends, slowly advancing my purpose. But like a young bird, I knew there was always a moment when I'd be pushed from the nest. *Will I fly, or will I fall?* I'm pacing in Micah's anteroom. I know it's not calming me but I can't stop it. The tram is on the way.

"There can be echoes, you should be aware of that darling. The host's memories can rise up in extreme circumstances," Micah says, and I ignore him.

This is where Micah receives his clients, it's spacious and tasteful. Plush brown leather couches surround a coffee table on one side of the room, and a beautifully polished antique espresso machine is set up next to it with a row of miniature white cups. The other side of the room is dominated by full length mirror booths that allow you to see every angle of yourself. The floor is covered with tiny tiles, a beautiful mosaic in black and white. The beauty and calmness only expands my anxiety until it's bouncing off the too high ceilings and echoing with each tap of my boots on the floor.

"It might be wise to avoid excess alcohol too, seems your Allen was a bit of a partier, and those urges tend to stick around," he continues.

Last night, I pored over the files Micah gave me, unable to sleep as I imagined what might happen in the next moments, the next weeks, the next months. I understand Allen's family, my family, but it feels superficial. They're real people, not a page in a document that I can memorize, and it terrifies me. I've gambled my existence and my future on this, and I can't falter.

"Those strong memories will all settle down as you get more used to him, though. It just takes a bit longer to fully incorporate."

I've transferred the majority of the credits I had to Micah to cover the work he's done, and the recovery from it. The rest I sent to my mother, through Brian of course, as an inheritance from my death. I wish it would ease the burden, but I know it won't. Micah has helped me gain access to Allen's accounts now, so there's no use for the credits that got me this far. As I stare down at my screen, I see it recognizes me as him, and the sum of money tied to my new name seems completely irrational.

Micah says something else, but I miss it.

"What's that again, chap?" I finally pause in my pacing and face Micah. My heart is racing.

He looks as nervous as I feel. "There's something else important you need to know, before the tram gets here. My information hasn't always been perfect. I don't think anyone knows of Allen's untimely passing, but there's always a chance." He's rushing to spew this out, and from the lights that are playing over the anteroom now I can tell that the tram is landing outside.

"You're telling me this now?! Dammit Micah, what the hell does that mean?"

"Just keep your eyes open, don't be a fool, and be ready to take *preventative measures.*" At this, he hands me a package. It's a box the length of my forearm, thin and only as wide as my hand, wrapped extravagantly in shiny gold and purple. I take it from him and stare dumbly at it as the door flies open behind me.

I turn sharply, too fast, and startle a well-dressed porter who is holding the door open. He recovers, and bows deeply to me. "Sir Allen, what a pleasure to see you again. The family was starting to grow concerned—" Seeing my wild eyes and sweat on my brow he pauses, "Is all as it should be, sir?"

I comb my memory, and the name Joseph Meadowhearth surfaces. *No older relatives, one daughter, friendly character, family has been porters to mine for generations.* I relax my face and give him my best heir-quality smile. "All good, chap, just coming down from a few medical things. Great to see your mug again, Joe. Any chance you brought any of the family with you?" I need to know what I'm walking into.

"No, sir, the hovercar is empty, as you prefer. They await your arrival in Cloud Spire."

"Good man, that's for the best. I need a few moments to breathe before we get there is all." Turning back to Micah, I jut out my hand officiously. "It's been a treat as always, Michalengelo, your reputation is well earned." We shake hands, and I give him a playful wink. Then I turn and follow Joe out of the shop.

Outside, I am overwhelmed immediately by the luxurious hovercar parked on the promenade. Transportation needs are limited in the city, and it's almost certainly faster to walk in the lower levels, so I've never been in one. I'd see them darting through the night sky, always too fast to see clearly, a world apart from my understanding. Shiny metal, glass, and sleek lines dominate the exterior—it looks like a skyscraper replica made miniature. Glass covers the entire cabin, allowing a panoramic view when you're above the city, or at the flick of the switch it can become clouded to offer privacy. Lush purple lounge seats line both sides of the cabin, which is fully separated from the cockpit.

With a start, I realize that Joe is holding the door to the cabin open for me and likely has been for some time. Lowering my head, I climb into the cabin and sink into the rear seat. Comfort soothes me instantly. I close my eyes and breathe deeply, and Joe clicks shut the door behind me. Sound from outside is instantly muffled, and a faint jazz music plays from hidden speakers. Music is so rare these days, and the commonality of it playing in the cabin of a tram for a solo passenger astounds me.

Joe speaks to me through an intercom in the cockpit. "Straight to the house then, master Allen?"

"Let's take a cruise around the city first. I want to see the lights, Joe." This was a common request from Allen, and I can tell that Joe was anticipating it.

"Of course, sir, I'll turn off the opacity once we get a little higher." I realize at this that we're already in the air, but take-off was so smooth it didn't even register.

In another few moments, there's a soft click that seems to come from every surface around me. As if they're dissolving, all of the exterior surfaces slowly turn translucent. My stomach drops at the distance beneath my feet, and I have to quell a sudden urge to vomit. The city sleeps ten stories beneath us, sprawling in every direction. It's beautiful from up here, a carpet of lights, but the distance makes it feel trivial. Other cars zoom around us, and for an instant I see into the lives of their passengers. This one reading the paper, that one putting on make-up, another couple that's arguing. It's a whole life that I never knew existed, down on the ground, and it sucks me in.

As we climb higher, the scale of the city comes into view, and it draws a sharp contrast to the walls that line it. Five Boroughs and Meadow Hearth cover a massive swath of land, but from up here in miniature their defining visual trait is the abrupt end at the circular wall of the city. The higher we climb, it's harder to see the specifics of those places. From up here, only the sprawling towers and the edges of the city seem to matter.

We're in a procession of hovercars that are circling the towers of Cloud Spire. They must rise a hundred stories off the ground. Each level has a landing pad, and several have external structures that pock the exterior surface of the tower. Massive open-air gardens, fully glass swimming pools, and other niceties cantilever from the building's sides to support the taste of the uber wealthy. Trams are constantly spiraling inwards to land, or lifting off to join the swirling mass. In the distance, I can see the mega structures of Sun Gate—they somehow still dwarf all this.

A tram suddenly swerves towards us, and Joe takes immediate evasive maneuvers. We dive and twist, tossing me against the harness that holds me to the cushioned seat, and the other car breezes over our side without colliding. I swirl around and catch a glimpse of the driver howling in laughter and glee, his eyes are wild and bloodshot. The car continues its upward trajectory through the swirling mass, almost hitting two others before it shoots out into unoccupied air and dives toward the city.

From his side profile, I see Joe mutter something in distaste.

"What a buffoon. Thanks for the quick moves, Joe."

"Aye, sir. Luna took a toll on that one," he says pointedly, and I surmise that Joe knows of Allen's bad habits.

"A distasteful state, it really is robbing our best and brightest. I know I've had my own past with it, but I'm a new man now."

"Happy to hear that, sir, and I'm sure the family will be very pleased to hear it as well. My little Josephine is a big fan of yours, and I'd hate to tell her you went down the drain like those users."

"Ahhh, how is the little tyke now?" I say, smiling. Memories flood me of Allen giving a ride on his back to a young girl at a family party while she laughs gleefully.

"Taller and brighter by the day, probably the smartest girl our family has seen. She'll be taking the job from her old man any day now" Joe says proudly, and I can see him smiling now.

There's something special here, something I wasn't expecting. Joe and his family seem to be an integral part of my family, even though they're only from Meadow Hearth. For generations, our two lines have been intertwined, and seemingly with mutual respect. I wonder how Joe views it.

Shaking me from my thoughts, Joe says, "ready to land now, sir?"

"Let's go home. I have to face them at some point."

Joe nods, and pilots the car to a higher level. We're climbing towards the top of the tower, and I wonder how high up there *home* is. I look down at the package sitting in my lap that Micah gave me, and feel a sudden itch to tear it open. We circle closer to the magnificent tower, all polished metal and glass, until at the tenth floor from the top Joe expertly flicks the car around and reverses onto a landing pad.

The house behind us is massive, it would easily swallow a city block of houses in Five Boroughs. It stretches upwards with twenty-foot high ceilings, and all the edges gleam polished silver. A garden is suspended off to one side, and opposite that are some smaller private balconies that must adjoin different rooms of the house. Some of the glass, which covers every surface, has been turned transparent, and behind the windows I see a shining magnificence that makes my imagination feel petty. There's a kitchen the size of my family home with two cooks working, and in another room a hand-carved wooden table with matching high-backed chairs that stretches to a comical length. I see a room dominated by a massive bed, and a woman standing in the window sees the car land and hurries to the front entrance.

I'm an alien on pilgrimage to an unknown land, and when we land I just want to ask Joe to take me back. Take me away from here, leave me in the Boroughs with the people I know and the comfort of barely scraping by, of looking out for one another.

But he's pulling the door open for me, and I'm mechanically swinging out of the car to meet this life head on.

The woman from the house is running towards the car. She's a classic beauty with shoulder length blonde hair and curves that pop from her high-waisted dress. As she's running to me, everything is flouncing and bouncing. I think at first this must be Allen's sister from her age, but the documentation said he didn't have one, and as she draws near I realize this is his *mother*. Alicia Cloudspire. Supposedly she's in her 50s, but I don't see a single sign that she continued to age past 30. *I wonder how much time she's spent with Micah.*

She reaches me and throws her arms around me, crying into my chest. I mechanically put my arms around her with Micah's present still clutched in my left hand.

"Hullo, Mother, I've returned."

"Allen, we thought, you've been gone so long, oh hell I thought something terrible happened." She gets out around her sobs. She hugs me fiercely and then separates herself. At arms distance now, she stares into my eyes. "Oh, your eyes! What a marvelous shade of green you chose. Sweetheart, if you wanted to get some work done you know you didn't have to hide it from us. Your mum could have given you some advice, you know. We were so worried about you! Why didn't you call us? Your father will be so relieved to see you." All this rushes out of her, like a faucet that's been flipped to full open. I look over her shoulder to see the silhouette of a man standing in the doorway, smoking a pipe.

"Let's go see dad," I say, and she takes my arm as we walk back to the house. My father is a muscular, regal man. As we get closer, I see his gray hair is cut short and he sports a tightly cropped beard. Allen Sr. is a firm man who enjoys his smoking pipe and neat whiskey, but as we get close enough I can see that he's crying. I let go of Mom's arm and hug him, and he hugs me back tighter than I ever expected.

"I'm glad you're okay, son. You gave us quite a scare. Where the hell have you been, anyways?"

I put a hand on each of their shoulders. "I've been recovering at Michelangelo's, but not just from his work. I had a close call with Luna, and I'm off the stuff for good. I'm sorry I scared you two, I just needed to find myself again."

My mom makes a small choking noise at this, and hugs me again. My dad piles onto the hug afterwards too. It's a touching moment, but it's not mine. There's a small pang of guilt for the betrayal, for the fact that they're hugging a walking corpse of their son, but I remind myself that these bastards deserve it. *People like this prop up the whole system, they think it's normal and fair. They're complicit and I can't let myself forget that.*

"Let's go inside and have some dinner. We heard you were coming and the cooks have been working all day on a celebration meal. Charon will be delighted to see you too, I'm sure," my dad says. For a moment, I freeze at the name. It resonates with something in my new memories, but nothing concrete comes up.

With their arms on my back, we walk into the house, and as the door clicks shut behind me I know my fate is sealed. Wherever this road leads, I'm on it now and there's no turning back.

CHAPTER 5

The house is stunning, and I have to constantly remind myself not to gawk, not to give away that I'm in awe of everything around me. The ceiling, twenty feet up, is covered in a tasteful mixture of mirrors, hand painted frescoes, and chandeliers that simultaneously make the rooms feel infinite and classic. There are noise disruptors built into the walls, so no matter how loud you are there's never an echo, and every conversation sounds intimate. Majestically thick carpets and hardwood cover the floors. Wood is very rare in the city so this display of wealth immediately makes me blanch. Every room seems to be a new treat, a feast for the eyes and senses.

Before exploring the house, I make my way to Allen's bedroom. The space is massive and spartan. There are no personal touches visible, and the room is dominated by a massive bed and impressive closets on either side with mirrored doors. At the back of the room a glass door exits onto a personal balcony, and in the corner next to it is a shower covered in wrap-around glass paneling.

I set Micah's package down on the bed, and after thinking on it, decide to tuck it underneath the pillow. I'll open it later, when I get some time alone. Then I move to the closets. I've been wearing a suit jacket and shirt recovered near Allen's body all day, and it feels vile. The mirrored doors slide noiselessly open as I approach, and I stare at a row of tuxedos, suit jackets, ties, vests, and silk shirts. Up to this point, I wore one of two high durability jumpsuits every day and never thought about my clothing. Half of these articles of clothing don't even make sense to me how to wear, and I realize this is a massive oversight in my training.

As I'm contemplating this, and wondering what I can learn quickly from my screen, two spindly robotic arms separate themselves from the top of the closet and grab my sleeves. My first response is to fight them off, but as I twist away from them they simply lift off my suit jacket, and then come back to unbutton my shirt. Realizing they are likely just trying to be helpful, I stop squirming and leave my arms elevated.

The arms remove my clothing and deposit them internally, likely for some laundry service. One of the arms comes back to show me my upcoming schedule on an integrated screen, it reads *Family Celebration Dinner*, and I nod in affirmation. The arms then go to work picking out new clothes, and pulling them on me as I assist minimally. In five minutes, I'm dressed in a shiny new tuxedo with an iridescent purple bow tie. The fabric is wonderfully soft against my skin, and I only now realize how coarse my old jumpsuits were. At the end, I'm offered some accoutrements for my outfit, one arm holds up a bowler hat, and the other a matching purple pocket square. I motion towards the pocket square, and it's folded neatly into my tuxedo.

What world is this where I'm to put on a tuxedo for a family dinner? I leave my bedroom to explore the rest of the house.

To the right of the main entrance as you enter the house is the dining room, the centerpiece of entertaining. It's dominated by a massive oak table that easily seats twenty. Plants adorn the walls and floor at regular intervals, making the room feel alive and dynamic. I haven't been around this many plants before, and as I pace the length of the table it's intoxicating to me how fresh the air is. A large double door at the opposite end opens out into the garden, and from here I can see that between the towering plants and trees there are gazebos and discreet benches for large parties, or potentially for sneaking away from them. A memory floats up of the whole area bustling with dinner guests, drunkenly running around like children through the greenery, and then it fades away again. I leave exploring the garden for later and exit back into the house.

To the left of the main entrance is the library. All printed books are antiques, and I've never seen a collection so massive. The room has an amplified quiet from discreetly placed noise canceling devices that makes you want to sink into the low, comfortable chairs scattered tastefully around the room. The smell of aged parchment is intoxicating and beautiful. These books have survived from a history that I don't even know, and I want to sit down and read each of them.

I meet Charon there, and he is decidedly *not* happy to see me. As I'm walking down the aisle of books, reading titles I've never heard of, a shadow separates itself from one of the armchairs. It stretches lazily, arching its long back, and walks slowly towards me. Icy panic rushes through me, I've never seen a creature like this before, made fully of darkness, and I back away slowly. As he steps into the light from one of the reading lamps, I understand that the moving shadow I saw is a massive black cat. His body is half the size of mine, and although his movements are graceful and refined, they hold a deadly quietness to them.

Pets, even small ones, are not common in the city, they're an extravagance that no one can afford. I've only seen panthers in historical photos on my screen. I didn't think anything like this existed in the city. As he draws himself into the light, I see that there's a small box attached to the collar around his neck.

Charon stops a couple of feet from me, and sits on his haunches. *You are not him. You are a lie.* The voice hisses out of the box from around his neck as he raises a fat paw and cleans his claws, and I realize that it's translating. For a moment, I only gape at him.

I look around to make sure I'm alone in the room, and then whisper, "I'm not him, but I am not dangerous, I'm friendly. I can be a friend to you too, if you would like." There is no fooling this cat, the best I can do is take a chance.

Charon stares at me, unblinking and unmoving. I wonder if I could protect myself from this cat, and how sharp and long his claws are. At the end of an eternity of waiting, Charon decides something, and walks out of the room slowly and deliberately, not even sparing a glance at me. I stand completely still the entire time, sweat pouring down the back of my neck.

Alicia finds me in the library soon after. I'm still jumpy from the encounter with Charon, so when she speaks behind me I nearly crawl out of my skin.

"Darling, the celebration dinner is prepared. Will you come join us in the dining room? The cooks have made *all* of your favorite dishes." She's wearing a low cut, high-waisted black dress with the same iridescent purple accents as my tuxedo.

With her, the smells of food waft in, and when they hit my nose my stomach clinches into knots like I've been punched. These are smells wholly new to me, spices in the air that are delicately rich, sweet, and savory. The symphony is beautiful as it dances across me and pulls me in.

"Of course, mum, just picking out a bedtime story. Any recommendations?" She grabs a slim volume off the shelf and hands it to me. The title *The Sun Also Rises* is stamped in gold leaf on the cover.

"I've always liked this one, what fun they have, but I don't think I ever finished it. Maybe you will, darling."

I take it, feeling the delicacy of the paper and leather binding, and follow her out of the room.

In the Boroughs, meals consist of blocks, served in one way or another. They're a kind of nutrient dense food made in Sun Gate that can be cooked any way you want, all of them are equally bad. Some people use printers to make them look like other, real foods, but most don't have the patience. Real spices are a luxury that no one can afford, so synthetic flavoring packs are the only thing we had to make it palatable. Getting enough food down there only meant that you weren't losing weight anyways. Everyone was hungry.

Until this night, I'd had real food only twice in my life. The first was the night I took my first job, and my father took me out for a bowl of noodles in Meadow Hearth to celebrate. It was mostly broth, but the few noodles in the bowl were thick, chewy, and the most filling thing I'd ever had. The second was the night before my father took the job that devastated him, as we celebrated one last time with the advance on his final paycheck. We had real meat from a tin then, a small sliver for each of us, and I still remember the salty and savory flavors.

What I walk into in the dining room makes me salivate instantly, and it shames me. The table is laid with a spread of foods that I only recognize half of. Baked potatoes, charred asparagus, a centerpiece of roasted duck—actual real duck—and several other dishes are ready to serve. The sight of it makes me dizzy, and I grab the back of a chair to steady myself. Enough food for twenty people easily, but it's meant only for the three of us. A hundred feet below me, down in the Boroughs, my mother is making another tasteless meal of blocks, and the thought of it tears at my heart.

Here, my mother is flitting around directing the wait staff where to put more dishes, and what the order will be for food service. The head chef listens to her, nodding and taking notes on her screen.

My father comes in behind me and puts his hand on my shoulder. I look back at him, dressed in a similar tuxedo to mine.

There's a beautiful carved pipe in his pocket, inlaid with shining purple that sparkles against the dark wood grain. "It's good to have you back, my boy."

I smile at him, and my mother floats back to the table gracefully. Seats are pulled out for us by the wait staff, and as we sit, our plates are prepared with food and placed in front of us.

"Oh darling, you just must try these new kill-cal pills," my mother says, pulling a small metal tin out of her ample decolletage and showing me small white pills inside.

I look down at them quizzically as my father takes one and swallows it. "What are they for mum?"

"Only the newest wonder product to come from the medical geniuses in Sun Gate. The pills stop your body from absorbing calories beyond exactly what your body needs. Now I don't take them at every meal, but sometimes a person just wants to keep eating and not worry if it's a bit *excessive*, you know?"

I stare at her, and at the pills, and I'm so flabbergasted that I don't even know what to say. A hundred feet below us, people are living on the edge of starvation on a subsistence diet of nutrition cubes, and here...

Realizing I've been quiet for too long, I manage to get out, "No thanks, mum, I'm famished! I want the full impact of my gluttony tonight."

She nods and puts the pill container back down the neckline of her dress.

We start with a course of charred asparagus, they're spiraled gracefully on our plates into an upside down funnel with a coarse salt sprinkled on top. The taste is exquisitely rich, and the insides are a perfect balance of crunch and give that is joyous to chew. By the first bite, I'm salivating uncontrollably, and by the second, my eyes have started to tear. Wine is served to pair with the plate, a sparkling dry thing. I take a controlled sip, and the flavor nearly takes my breath away.

"I say, Allen, have you heard about Darius?" my father asks probingly. There's a depth to his question. It grabbed my mother's attention and I don't know why. Darius Cloudspire, the son of Darius Sr. and Darlene, is Allen's friend. There wasn't much of him in the file from Micah, he's an occasional drinking partner from my understanding.

"What's that rake up to these days?" I ask, jokingly.

My father takes a swallow of wine and pats his mustache dry with a crisp napkin. "Well the rumor is his parents are trying to buy a Sicko to take on his addiction and—"

"Darius has always had something dark inside him, I'm sorry, dear," my mother says to me, consolingly.

"Righto, and no one even knows if the disease transfer machine can do that or not," my father finishes.

Some poor fool will try to take their money and find out, I'm certain of it.

"You know, if you ask me, that whole family is on their way down. Why, I wonder if they'll even be Cloudspires in a few generations! We heard, and darling, don't spread this rumor any further, but we heard they might have to sell their family home and move further down the tower to afford it."

"Of course Darius Sr. has his *predilections* that certainly don't help their financial affairs," my father adds gruffly.

Even I catch this one. From the file, Darius Sr. seems to be purely motivated by boozing, whoring, and gambling.

I shrug, and put on a placating smile. "Well either way I hope that chap gets what he needs, and not what he wants for once. I walked away from that life, maybe he can do the same."

My mother and father nod at my words, as if there's some secret wisdom hidden in them. As we've been chatting our meal has been replaced, and it took severe restraint not to grab the waiter's arm to stop him from taking my remaining food. The baked potatoes from earlier have been mashed and pressed into a mold so that they roughly resemble the city itself. A brown gravy was poured down it, and it ran down all the streets, and down to the Boroughs where it pooled. The gravy barely touches the molded towers of Cloud Spire and Sun Gate. Of course, my wine is swapped to a better pairing. Across the table my parents guzzle down the rest of their first glasses before handing them to the waiters.

"I say, what a unique presentation." I look around the miniature at different angles while sipping my new glass of red wine. The oaked cherry flavors blast my tongue and threaten to make me cry.

My mother is tickled by this. "I'm so glad you think so, dear. I've been working with the cooks on this for the last several weeks. You know I've always *loved* playing with my food."

With my first bite, I intentionally take down the miniature Sun Gate tower, and dip it into the gravy in the Boroughs. The potatoes are exquisite, they're rich and silky, and complemented by the delightful mushroom gravy. Not wanting my dish to be taken away before I'm done, I take greedy spoonfuls.

"Why, I see you still love potatoes, son. I remember when you were a young tyke that's all we could get you to eat some nights!" my father says, chuckling.

I rinse the potatoes down with a large draught of wine and smile. "Aye sir, guilty as charged."

We've made our way to the duck now, and the smell wafting from the freshly sheared leg on my plate is indescribable. I'm full already, but my stomach still rumbles in pleasure at the dish. A darker wine is served, it's as meaty and bodied as the duck. A pleasant buzz rings in my head now. I've never drunk this much wine before and I feel wonderful.

From the corner of my eye, I see Charon's shadowy form slink into the room and go underneath the dining table. I grab the leg of duck from my plate, and hold it out next to my knee. *I hope I still have my hand after this.* With a sudden violence, Charon grabs the leg from my hand. His sharp fangs slide past my hand as he does so, and it makes my stomach drop in cold terror. Underneath the table, Charon sits down on my feet and I can feel every muscle of him moving as he tears into the duck leg.

"Dear, now you really must stop feeding him from the table! While you were gone, he was practically begging for the food from our plates. And to give him the whole leg, why I hope he at least appreciates the flavor," my mother says smiling. She signals to the waiters, and they bring another plate for me, this time with duck breast.

My hand is still shaking as I cut off a bite from the duck, no matter how I try to hold it steady. "Ah, mother, but you know

I've always preferred breast meat," I say, motioning towards the duck breast.

Smirking, my father responds, "How we know it, son, and speaking of, how is Dorothy Sungate these days?"

I blush fiercely at the comment, only then realizing what I had said.

My mother guffaws at this, but slaps my father's arm. "Now don't be lewd, darling. You know Dorothy comes from a very *respectable* family." Turning back to me, she says, "But I do think the two of you were quite a pair, and what a thing that would do for our family! To have you match with a Sungate...why your father and I couldn't hope for better."

I'm sensing an opportunity here. Dorothy, or Dotty to her friends, is my potential link to get inside Sun Gate, and I need to bring her to my side. "Unfortunately, I had a bad habit that pushed her from me, but who could blame her for that? I'm hoping to rekindle things when I can show her the new man I am."

"Why dear, I'm sure she'll swoon just when she sees those new green eyes you have. And we have the perfect opportunity." She claps her hands together, smiling. Her and my father share a look and then she continues. "Now we know that you just got back, and we don't want to overwhelm you, but we're planning a ball in a week's time—"

"Just a few families invited, an intimate affair, nothing outlandish," my father assuages.

"Right, just a few hors d'oeuvres and glasses of wine with friends. But of course we'd be honored to invite Dotty and her family! All to grow the seed of *young love*." My mother finishes by putting her hands over her heart and batting her eyes at my father, who winks at her.

I chortle. "We're not that young anymore mum, but still, it would be fantastic to see her again. I'll look forward to the ball then."

I realize now that as we've been talking I haven't been eating my duck, and this is something that I will not let go to waste. I skewer the first succulent bite and put it in my mouth, and the flavor is explosive. Salty, caramelized meat dances around my palate—it overwhelms everything I am, and before I can hold anything back I'm crying.

"Oh honey, what's wrong? Have we upset you?" my mother asks, concerned by my outburst.

"The duck, it's magnificent," I get out, drying my eyes with my napkin. My mother looks fit to burst with pride and happiness.

My father bursts into laughter. "The young lad's been eating street vendor trash for too long, he's forgotten where he comes from!" After a piercing glare from my mother he adds, "But dear it is magnificent, of course."

When dinner is done my head is swimming from the richness and the wine. I need to find my way to bed, I think dimly, but the waiters are placing a whiskey nightcap in front of us. The strong smell reaches into my nostrils and wakes my brain back up. *Not bed you ponce, I need more, I'm just getting started. Pour me another barman, and find me some fucking Luna.* The thought arcs through my mind like a flash of lightning.

I feel a sudden, insatiable lust for oblivion. It feels foreign, but also familiar. Realization hits me then that these are not my own feelings, but a memory of Allen's surfacing. I clench my clammy palms into fists and try to focus back on the night, but it won't recede. The edges of my vision grow dark. *Give me more, give me more, give me more.* It echoes through my head, each reverberation causes a lancing pain behind my eyes. Distantly, I feel sweat beading on my forehead, and hear the voice of my mother reaching out to me.

"Darling, are you okay? You look like you're in pain!" Through my closed eyes I hear her stand and start to walk around the table to me.

Focus, these are just memories. Don't push them away, accept that they're a part of you, but they're not the whole of you. I let out a large exhale, and feel my pulse start to drop back down. Just as quickly as the feeling came on, it recedes. The thought of living with that need for destruction sends a shudder down my spine.

I open my eyes and stare up at her, and force a smile. She's standing next to me now, concern knitting her brow as she stares down at me. "Sorry about that, just some sudden indigestion. My body must be too used to that street food!" My father chuckles at this, and it clears the air. My mother's face smooths.

We grab our glasses and retire to the garden as the wait staff cleans up behind us. Charon trails at our heels, slinking in the shadows and pretending he's not following us. The veranda is magnificent and wipes all thoughts of Allen from my mind. I'm glad it's dark here because between the wine and the beauty, I'm crying freely. I grew up surrounded by trash, concrete, and sick humans. No one had the time or energy for plants. And here I'm standing now, engulfed by living things I have no name for. Some tower overhead, some dangle majestic vines. Beautiful flowers line all the beds in intricate colored patterns, their blooming scent fills the air.

We all move toward the balcony edge, where we can see the city sprawling underneath us. I'm surrounded by so much beauty, it's hard to remember to be angry about the condition of life down there. Instead, I'm just seeing the expanse of lights that twinkle in and out. It blends with the night sky that's shown on our city walls.

My father pulls out his ornate pipe, packs it with tobacco from a pouch, and lights it. The smoke is thick and cloying, and I stand outside of it to not choke.

"It really is beautiful up here," I say, half to myself.

"Of course it is, son. This is what we've earned with our position." My father sweeps his arm to gesture at the view.

"It would be so sad to be down there in the thick of it, unable to see above it," my mother says, taking a sip from her whiskey as she stares down. She seems to mean it too, there's real empathy in her voice, but I doubt she can really picture it.

"Don't worry dear, with our wealth this family's position is established for generations. There's only so much room up here though, and there's always got to be someone at the bottom of it. We all have our place."

I'm drinking my whiskey, listening to them. I think it's delicious, but the taste is reaching my brain from some distance so I can't be certain. I think I'm angry about what my father is saying, but I can't be certain about that either. I'm thinking through a cloud. I'm unstable, euphoric and soaring, but confused. Suddenly, my stomach lurches and twists into a knot, and before I can stop myself I lean over the balcony and vomit uncontrollably.

My father pats my back after I've finished. "Ahhh son, I could tell you were having a bit too much there. That's okay, it happens to the best of us."

My mother grabs my arm. "Come with me darling, we'll get you to bed." She leads me back to my room. The sudden nausea dissipates after vomiting, but I'm still stumbling. She puts me in front of the closet, and leaves the room as the robot arms help to undress me. I take a shower in the corner of my room, assisted by another pair of robot arms that scrub and then dry me. Then I plod my way on shaky legs to the soft looking bed.

The bed hits my shins, and I fall into it, face down. The pillow punches me back when my face lands though, and I remember vaguely that I put Micah's present under it. Seeing that I'm alone now, I pull the package out and open it.

I stare at what I find, uncertain what it is. It's a tube the length of my forearm with straps coming off at regular intervals. There's a note from Micah in his gracefully flamboyant handwriting. *Be careful darling, it's sharp.* I pick the item up, it looks like something that mounts to my arm. I test the fit against my right arm, and the straps around it come to life and wrap around me. They cinch down, and then the whole thing blends into my skin. I can't see it, but as I run my fingers over that arm I can feel their ridges.

I flex my wrist backwards, and a long plasma knife springs out from under my arm, sizzling in the air. I leap back from it in fear, and hit my head against the bed frame. Suddenly, I'm completely sober. When I move my wrist back, it disappears.

I test it again, and find the angle at which it leaps out. It's far enough back that it would be difficult to do accidentally, but I'll need to keep that in mind.

"Holy shit, Micah. What did you think I was getting into?" I mutter under my breath. But then I realize, he might have a much better idea than I do.

I throw the packaging on the ground, and lay my head back down on the pillow. The lights turn off automatically as I do, and my brain drifts. Somewhere in the middle of the night, a shadowy form lurks through the door and jumps up onto my bed. I wake more fully as I realize that Charon is sleeping at the foot of the bed, and I smile. Apparently, he must have enjoyed the duck. I fall back into a deep, dreamless sleep.

CHAPTER 6

I spend the next week living monastically. The morning after our family dinner, I find a gym and treadmill at the back of the house. There's a pool there too, but it seems better suited to drinking and lounging than physical conditioning. In the connected bathroom, I find a strange bed with a metal lid that fully covers it. It hinges open smoothly to show off plush, purple cushioning on the inside. Searching for the product on my screen, I find that it's designed to massively speed up muscle regeneration and growth.

With a tool like this, as long as I get enough calories and protein, I can train nearly non-stop. I don't know what I'll face or what I'll have to overcome if I ever make it into Sun Gate. I'm not a fighter, besides the little bit I learned at Micah's, but I figure that strength has practical uses beyond violence. I find a newer fighting drone in the corner of the gym for when violence is required.

My days start with paging the kitchen for a nutrient dense breakfast. I eat it while reading a book from the library and drinking a cup of coffee. The food is often new to me, but it's always delicious. The books are new and strange, with intoxicating ideas and scenes set in places I don't understand. I like one full of Greek myths the most, they're understandable parables and the settings are malleable. They don't mention a world that existed somewhere else, before the city. The idea of that makes me feel strangely woozy.

After that, I spend six hours running, sparring with the combat drone, lifting weights, and sitting in the regen bed. The work is hard at first, but I soon find myself luxuriating in the feeling of having a strong body. I flex at the mirror in the bathroom and watch my new, growing muscles ripple. The practice with the drone also helps me learn my new body quickly, and the force readout from the drone shows I'm drastically improving in the economy and power of my blows.

I pause my training only for a high calorie lunch, which I take on the veranda that adjoins the library. In the artificial sunlight, the city looks much different than it does at night, when the darkness cloaks everything in beauty and twinkling lights. During the day, the city looks dirty and malformed, with a haze that drifts up from the sewers and settles over the Boroughs. The seams in the wall are clear from here, I can focus and see the gaps in the panels of the artificial sky. *Rise too high and you'll see the gaps in the sky, shall I also singe my wings by getting too near the sun?*

The night after our family dinner, my father joins me on the veranda for his lunch. He spends most of the day shut in his office. From what I can hear from the door, he orchestrates buying goods for one price, and then selling them for a higher price. There's yelling and bartering involved, like a shopkeep that plays puppet master to all the city's shopkeeps.

"Training for a war in there, son?" my father asks as he sits down with me. A waiter trailing him sets down a tray of lunch and sparkling mineral water, bows, and leaves.

If only he knew how close to true that is. "I've discovered there's a great joy to be found in growing myself, father. I'm planning to spend my days training my body and my mind, it's wonderful to focus on something like that instead of destroying myself."

At this he nods, and takes a contemplative bite from his lunch. He takes a sip from his mineral water, and pats his mustache dry with a pristine, white napkin.

"When I was young—younger than you are now actually—my father died. Did you know he had died so early? Stabbed by another Cloudspire jealous of his position. It was such a waste. I raged against the world, and myself, after that. I thought I'd drown in my depression, most days I wanted to. I spent nearly all of them dangerously drunk, picking fights in Meadow Hearth. I lived for the days when I would find another Cloudspire down there, and get a chance to pummel them. For a time there was only the drink, and the destruction.

"And when I look back at it now, I see someone that was hurt by the world, and wanted to hurt it in return. When you're young, passions and anger come so easy, everything is so visceral. I'm telling you this so you know that I understand being self-destructive, but there's no way to heal by doing it. Your mother pulled me out of that actually, but that's a story for another time. I'm so happy to see you growing yourself instead of destroying yourself."

I'm shocked by the sympathy in his tone. Here is a man that ardently believes society is laid out appropriately, and feels no remorse for those on the lowest rungs, but he shows such an understanding for his son. There's more humanity up here than I expected, and it makes me feel another pang of guilt for taking his son's place, for not letting this family properly grieve. But the amount of pain I'm causing here is nothing in comparison to the rampant suffering of the Boroughs. *I can't let this distract me.*

"Thank you, father. It's been a journey to get here, and I know it'll continue to be hard at times. But I've started to find joy in the process again, and the reward from that is immense."

He nods again, and finishes his lunch. Patting his mustache dry again, he says, "Well get back to it then, you've been resting for long enough!" At this he chuckles, and then returns to his work.

By the middle of the week, my body is noticeably more taut, and it bulges in new areas around my shoulders and chest. I'm in the middle of a particularly hard set of press exercises when a porter interrupts me.

"Sir, a letter courier at the door for you. He insists the letter must be handed directly to you." The porter sounds irritated at this, likely from having to interrupt me for what seems a trifle.

A letter? Who even knows I'm here at this point? I follow the porter back to the main entrance, wrapping a towel around my bare shoulders to mop up sweat on the way. The letter courier is sitting directly inside the front entrance, he has been allowed no further inside the house. He's a mouse of a man. Short with a jutting nose and a pinched face, his brown hair is tied back into an orderly ponytail.

The courier bows deeply before leveling indifferent brown eyes at me. "Sir Allen Cloudspire, a letter for you from my master, Darius Cloudspire." He extends his hand, in it a wax sealed envelope with an embossed *DC*.

Leave it to these Cloudspires to send wax sealed letters by courier when they could just as easily message each other on their screens. Showing some disdain, I snatch the letter from the courier and rip it open, placing the envelope into my porter's outstretched hands while I open the letter. It's wine stained, and the hand-writing comes from a shaking hand. *Darius is living up to his reputation so far, he must be a complete mess.*

Dear Friend,

I hear you've risen from the grave and returned to your familial home. I'm certain they're ecstatic for the return of the prodigal son. How proud of you they must be. I wonder what hole you disappeared into for so long, and just how cold you must have been.

I received an invite to your family's ball, I'm sure this is mostly an attempt by your vulpine mother to substantiate certain rumors floating around about my family. We shall be honored to take this invitation, and I cannot wait to see your smiling facade soon.

Warmest Wishes,
Darius

I stare at the letter, my hand trembling and breath caught in my chest. I feel chills running down my back as I reread the letter. *Fuck, he knows. He must know. And he's going to try and expose me.* I crumple the letter in my fist, and stuff it into my pocket as my resolve builds back.

I'm dimly aware that the courier has said something to me. I look back up to him. "What's that, man? Speak up."

He actually clicks his heels together, and straightens his back at my aggression. "Yes sir, shall you be writing a response?"

"Tell that buffoon that I'm a *new man*, and I'm not interested in *resurrecting* old friendships. If he knows what's good for him, he'll let this die. I will not write that message down, I expect you to deliver it verbatim." The courier colors fiercely at this slight against his employer, and after bowing, leaves hurriedly through the door.

My porter is smiling deeply at how I've dealt with the situation. "Thank you for your time, Master Allen."

I return to the gym with a renewed fury boiling inside me. My wrist is itching to flex and unleash the invisible knife paired to it, but I restrain myself in case someone sees. There's a rage inside me that I've never felt before. A churning thing that threatens to boil over and explode. I know it's Allen's anger seething in me, but instead of squashing it I lash my own righteousness to it and let it burn. *I will not be stopped by some drugged dilettante, what I'm doing is too important. If that fool rises against me, I will put him down.*

I take my lunch in the garden on the day before the ball. I've been dwelling on Darius's letter, and the thought of meeting Dorothy tomorrow night. A mixture of anxiety, hope, and fear swirls inside me as I walk into the garden, and sit at a sublime table that is shadowed by large ferns. Dappled sunlight streams through the leaves, sleepy by the time it reaches the pages of my book. There's a calmness rooted in this place. I breathe into it and feel my internal tension loosen.

A noise from the other side of the garden breaks my concentration, and I wonder who it could be. Someone is humming idly, peacefully as they work. It's a song I know, somewhere so deep inside myself that I can't place it. The song lifts me though, and forces a smile on my face. I set my book down on the table, and go to find who hums it.

I navigate meandering paths in the garden, coming upon several dead ends. The humming grows louder at times, and quieter at others as I move towards and away from the source. It's impossible to see over or through the dense foliage of the garden, so I strike out blindly along paths that I believe will take me there, only to lose my direction. The last path I try is lined with cherry trees in bloom and their smell overpowers everything. The air is thick and heavy with a flowery sweetness like honey. The path twists and turns, and then opens suddenly into a wide, patterned flower bed. My mother sits in the middle of it in a work-wear jumpsuit, dirt up to her elbows, and a wide brimmed hat on to shade her face. She looks up to me and smiles as I walk into the flower patch, careful not to step on anything.

"Hullo darling, you found me, the monster at the center of the maze," she says, setting down a hand spade and smiling at her own joke.

"Good afternoon, mum. What are you doing digging around in the dirt? Couldn't one of the house staff maintain the garden?"

She pats a stool near her, and I come to sit at her side. Turning to face me she says, "Darling, as a little girl I watched my mother tend to a flower bed and asked her the same thing. And she taught me that to care for these delicate beauties brings peace to the soul in a way that just observing them never can. It makes you pause, and help something so small that an errant step could end its life. I learned the craft from her, and when I miss her I come out here to work. I've always hoped that one day you'd show an interest, so I can show you the same peace."

I'm touched by it. This woman has wealth that I could not comprehend even months ago, she seems primarily driven by outward appearances and societal standing, but there is still some side of her that relishes this small joy.

"Well these clothes are already sweat soaked, so no harm in getting them dirty as well. What are you planting today?" I kneel in the dirt next to her and she smiles so warmly that my heart cracks open, and I smile back. She passes me a spade and we toil in the dirt together, planting new pink carnations.

"What was that song you were humming, mum?"

She smiles inwardly. "That was a tune that I sang to you when you couldn't sleep, and it's the same song my mother sang to me when I couldn't sleep. I don't know what it's called, the lyrics must have been forgotten long ago. But it's lovely all the same, I'm glad you recognized it."

It's a strange thing, these memories that float inside me. At times I feel like I am her son, at times I feel completely separate from this world.

We work together as the light fades, and she continues to hum.

As I lay in bed that night, I can feel something shifting inside me. There's a strangeness in this house that defies my expectations. I had vilified these people before I came here, and in large their passions and drive are what I expected. My mother's vanity, and my father's greed are what I anticipated finding. I did not expect to find their compassion and sympathy.

I wrestle with the duality of it. *Are they representative of this high society, or an anomaly? Could they be taught to not take advantage of the poor, could they be convinced to change society organically? Or are their other instincts too overwhelming? Is taking advantage of them wrong when the amount of injustice I could correct is so great?*

Charon is annoyed at my shifting around, and with a low growl he stands from his spot at the foot of the bed, stretches, and plops down away from my feet. I reach out and scratch his head, and he presses it firmly against my palm.

Go to sleep, it is late, his voice box hisses eerily in the dark room.

"You're right boy, and a big day tomorrow." I snap my fingers in the darkness, and a robotic arm delivers a small vial of sleeping solution to my waiting hand. I drink it down, and hand the empty container back to the darkness. And as I close my eyes, the world is already fading.

CHAPTER 7

The ball is decidedly *not* a small affair. Since before I rose, the house has been in commotion. Porters and wait staff decorate the rooms, stringing garlands and lights to set the mood. A new chandelier is installed in the main foyer, and for hours after I find myself admiring the way it gleefully tosses flashes of light. The cooks have been hard at work since dawn. The magnificent smells from them saturate the house until finally my mother orders all the windows and doors opened. She flits through it all, directing the commotion as her nightgown flutters around her shoulders like she's some matriarchal wraith.

Before guests arrived my father pulls me aside, two glasses of whiskey in his hand. "Best to stay out of the way in these situations my boy, why don't we retire to the veranda for a little warmer before the wolves get here?"

We sit on the balcony adjoining the library, whiskies in hand, staring down onto the city. My father packs and loads his pipe, and for a while we don't speak. The drink and smoke goes directly to my head, but the flavors are magnificent. Rich woodsmoke, caramelized sugar, and vanilla swirl on my tongue. I feel myself loosening, and realize that my anxiety had been steadily climbing as the time for guests to arrive got closer.

"How many do we expect tonight?"

My father chuckles. "Not even I know that privileged information, my boy. Kept close to her chest, you know how it is. Why, I bet she's invited half of the damn Cloud Spire tower, and a good contingent from Sky's Reach and Sun Gate. She really is puffed to have you back in the roost, so don't hold it against her if she wants to strut her plumage a bit."

I smile at this, the whiskey easing my concerns of what sort of performance I'll need to put on tonight. "Shall I wait at the door to greet guests as they arrive, then? The illustrious son, smiling and looking fit and healthy?"

"Now that would be a good move, I think your mother would approve. But only as you see fit to do so, make sure to get out there and mingle. This is a party for you after all, no need to play porter the entire night."

I nod, and we drain our glasses together. My father winks at me. "Make sure to get in a word with that Dotty of yours too, I hear she'll be coming accompanied by her father."

"Aye, sir. Mum won't be the only one strutting her feathers I guess," I say, smiling back at him.

He claps me on the back. "Well the time is coming close, let's go get dressed so the guests don't find us in our leisure wear."

My closet gives me the choice of two outfits for the evening, both are more casual than I anticipated. The first is a classic dark gray sports coat, but the seams have been embroidered with a thread so black it cancels out the idea of light. It's to be worn with a deep green shirt that perfectly compliments my eye color, and dark gray slacks. The other is an olive green jacket that's been bejeweled to shimmer in the light, and a black turtle-neck to wear underneath. *Couldn't it just be something simple.* I point to the sports coat.

The clothes fit astoundingly well, and must have been tailored to conform to my new, bulkier shape. They seem cut to accentuate my muscular frame, adding a nearly indecent amount of definition to every line of my body. As I'm inspecting the clothes, the arms come out of the closet and sculpt my loose curls of hair into a ponytail. As a last step, the arms spray something in both my eyes that deepens their color, and makes them shimmer slightly in the light. When I close my eyes, I still see the broken man coming to on Brian's hospital bed, rail thin and barely alive. But when I open them, I see the illustrious heir to a powerful family. *I look fit to rule a damn empire now.* It strengthens me.

When I exit my room, a small litany of guests are already here. I've learned enough at this point to know that anyone who arrives this early is looking to rise from a lower position, and is probably not worth my time. They flit around the house, talking overly loud to fill the mostly empty space while drinking copiously to cover their timidity. I ignore the small groups, and make my way to the front door.

My father and mother are by the door speaking to a guest. My father has chosen an outfit similar to mine, although his shirt is a deep blue to complement his eyes. My mother is in a modestly cut black gown that seems to barely contain her. It hugs to her frame and completely outlines her form. She wears a beautiful silver necklace with a massive sapphire that sits at her throat. As I get closer to them, I see that they're speaking with Micah, and I grin wholeheartedly as I approach.

Micah's outfit is a feast for the eyes with lavish purples, pinks, and silver trim at all the edges. His face is bedazzled with jewels, and he wears a top hat outlined with pink carnations.

"Oh Michelangelo, you remembered and wore my favorite flowers!" My mother says gleefully as I approach.

He bows towards her. "Anything to impress, my lady." As he rises, he sees me join the group, and bows deeply in my direction. "Monsieur Allen, it is good to see you again."

I ignore the formality and hug him fiercely, catching him off guard. I stand back and hold his shoulders. "It's good to see you again, my friend. And looking so flashy, as well!" I say, motioning towards his suit.

My parents smile at the exchange, knowing this man was with me during my *recovery* they are likely even more fond of him. More guests arrive behind him, and my parents move to greet them. I'm torn between needing to play a role in this family, and wanting to talk to my friend. He's the first person I've seen in so long that really knows me, and I want to cling to him like a life raft.

Micah winks at me and pats my arm. "Go say hi to them, darling. It really is good to see you again. *You've taken to this life well,"* he whispers as he squeezes my bicep and moves off into the house.

I go through a seemingly endless series of greeting guests, smiling, bowing, flashing smiles and batting eyes. Their names and faces blend together, a continuous stream of smartly dressed Cloudspires and Skysreachs who pamper me with compliments and comment on how beautiful my new eyes are. I am my family's heir, and I play the role well. My parents have long since moved into the crowd. Wine is flowing freely now, waiters walk around with trays of glasses and hors d'oeuvres, and a jovial fervor seems to permeate the air.

When Dorothy, and her father Dorian enter, they nearly take me by surprise. I'm trying to wrap up greeting a young Penelope Cloudspire, who is effusively telling me how happy she is to see me—and I believe flirting heavily with me—when they walk in. Like they have an increased gravity, the whole room seems to shrink towards them. As my attention is captured, Penelope sighs in frustration and moves into the room.

Dotty is so much more beautiful in person than in Allen's memories that I am nearly bowled over by it. Her hair is jet black, cut into a bob with short, blocky bangs that frame her angular face and rich hazel eyes. Her mouth is wide, with thick, red lips that smile involuntarily when she sees me. Where every other woman in the room wears something form fitting, she wears a luxuriously loose, white cashmere dress that hangs delicately, accentuating the curves of her body like water flowing over rocks. Her legs and bare arms are not thin and frail, but outlined with impeccably maintained muscle. The white dress seems to amplify her dark, bronze skin, and make the rest of us look pale and sickly.

For many moments I don't notice her father, but he is no less impressive. A tall, austere man with gray peppered hair and a deep cunning that twinkles in his pitch black eyes. He wears a dark gray suit that is barely accented by the black turtleneck underneath. He looks ready for a funeral. His dark skin is drawn across his angular, bony face, but in seeming contrast to his dour look, he smiles as he approaches me. He carries an antique cane crowned with a massive purple jewel, despite having no need for it. From what I know, he is a senior at the medical research facility in Sun Gate, and is the most powerful man I have ever met.

I bow deeply and slowly as they approach. "Welcome, it is our great pleasure to have you join us from Sun Gate."

"Allen, quit with the formalities, you know that I can't stand them." Her father reaches out and gives me a forearm handshake. This is the most intimate greeting that people from higher rungs will offer those from lower, and it is sure to be noticed by those in the crowd. He is smiling deeply at me. "Why your eyes, what a striking change!"

We release our grip and I turn to Dotty, she simply smiles and bows slightly, so I do the same. A memory of something inside me hungers to reach for her, to hold her, and the coldness of the greeting puts knots in my stomach.

"Allen, I hope you can add to a conversation my daughter and I were having on our way here. I think you were never quite infected by her neoprog politics—" As he's speaking, I signal to a waiter behind us and they serve us glasses of red wine. I move into the room with them, my time at the door is over. "You see, it is my lovely daughter's supposition that the rich, namely us my boy, prey upon the poor by using the disease transfer machine. Whereas I propose that this is life saving technology, and that everyone who uses it is a willing participant whose payment is driven by standard market forces. What do you think, Allen?"

"Oh father, you know that Allen has never been interested in politics, he's always cared so much more about things that make him *feel something*, and the poor have certainly never done that."

The jab cuts straight into my heart, but instead of showing my pain I smile sincerely at her. "Miss Dorothy, you wound me! It is true, there was a time in my not too distant past that I was motivated by more hedonistic pursuits, but I'm a different man now. I no longer stare at the moon looking for guidance, and with my eyes cleared, it's easy to notice the suffering of others."

Turning to her father, I say, "Sir Dorian, I believe that we ought not assign a value to the use of the disease transfer machine, as a base motivation all animals will do what's possible to extend their life and eliminate suffering. A better question might be if the societal mechanisms that separate the rich and poor are fair and just. Or, if the poor are 'willing participants' as you suggest, what forces push them to increase suffering, an action against our animal instincts, in their lives?"

At this, Dorian smiles and I see that cunning twinkle sparkle in his eyes. I can feel Dotty's gaze boring into me from the side. I know from their history that Allen's lack of political concern and copious use of Luna were the primary factors that drove a wedge between them. With my statement, I hope to extend a bridge back to her. She's the best avenue I have to gain access to Sun Gate, and maybe even the Medical Authority. I need her by my side.

"Why, Allen, your response shows wisdom that exceeds your class and age, well done. I see you must be finally making use of your father's impressive library. Speaking of, where is the man? I must thank him and your mother for inviting us to your lovely home, and hopefully grab a superb whiskey from their collection."

I turn around and point Dorian in their direction, and he thanks me as he leaves. As I turn back to speak to Dorothy, she has already closed the distance between us and we can now speak much quieter.

"Dotty, thanks for coming tonight. I've missed you deeply these months, and I just wanted to show you that I'm not the boy I used to–"

She puts her hand on my arm, and I quiet immediately. "There are not many who would differ in opinion from my father in public, and I appreciate the courage that took. But you must know that one statement will not make me believe your intent. I do hope that you're a changed man, Allen, but for your sake, not mine." She pauses here for a moment, staring into my eyes. "I do like your new eyes by the way, there's a humanity in them that was always absent before. Let's talk later on tonight." At this she walks into the crowd, and I watch people's gaze magnetically follow her as she walks away.

Over the next hours I mingle some with our guests, and sip sparingly on my wine, but it's hard to draw my heart into it. The pace of the party is increasing around me, and I can feel a drunken heat exuding from every pore of the crowd. After my last experience with alcohol, and Allen's memories that it surfaced, I want nothing to do with it. So from a sober distance, I watch them start to stumble, laugh too loud, and spill wine. Some guests have run off into the garden in pairs, looking for a discreet place to indulge themselves, or join in with other groups. The more exuberant everyone becomes, the more it amplifies the frivolity and waste, and it makes me wonder how my mother is doing in the Boroughs. Most guests are on the massive veranda at the back of our home, and I stand off to the side enjoying a view over the city by myself.

An arm suddenly sneaks up from behind and squeezes my bicep, and then links around mine as Dotty takes a position at the rail beside mine. My heart launches suddenly into my throat, and a happy anxiety roils inside me. She's close enough that I can taste the wine on her breath, and it's intoxicating.

She pulls in closer, and her breast presses against my arm. Instantly, a heady mixture of pleasure and fear races through me in response. "I must say, I do not mind this new bulk you've added. But I hope this *new man* you've become isn't just the type to darkly brood as he surveys *his kingdom*." At this she mockingly waves her hand across the expanse, and I laugh in response, but it comes out all high and wrong.

Is this wrong? I know I need to use her, I need to be cold here, but I don't feel cold. The thought of betraying her trust makes my guts clench in shame, but she's my only access to Sun Gate.

I need her. Still, I can't fully separate that need from these feelings that are racing through me. Old memories of Allen's and my own attraction seem to swirl together and make something totally new. Being near her makes it hard to focus on what I'm trying to do. Her proximity is the only thing I care about right now. *She seemed so hesitant earlier, I wonder why she's interested now.*

"So tell me, where did you hear all this stuff about societal mechanisms and *animal instincts*?" she asks me, lingering on the last two words.

I do not miss the emphasis, and I'm happy the light is at our back so she can't see my face color. "Ahh well you see, while I was recovering I had a great deal of time to think. There's something about near death experiences—" She stiffens at this, but I continue on, "—that gives you a chance to reflect on your own humanity. And during it all I was down there, in the thick of it, seeing how the other side lives. It changed me. So when I responded to your father, those were my own words. I truly believe in them."

She stares at me, quiet for some time and smiling sincerely. "I'm glad to hear it. I honestly thought the only self-reflection you were capable of was in a mirror."

At this joke, I laugh uproariously. I notice that she is drawing nearer to me, and I let her. She brings her hand up to stroke my hair, and I close my eyes and press against her hand. I feel a few strands of hair get pulled free, but keep focused on the sweetness of the moment. "I missed—"

"HHHEYYYYSHHHHHFUUUCCCKKKUUU!" From several paces away comes a guttural, drunken roar.

Both of us turn quickly to see a figure lumbering towards us across the balcony. The light is at his back, but I recognize the outline immediately: *Darius Cloudspire. Fuck, right now? I didn't even see him come in. Could there be worse timing? He must be completely drunk. What's his angle?*

He steps into the light, and it highlights the puke stains on the front of his black tuxedo. His normally curly dark hair is matted across his sweaty forehead, framing piercing blue eyes that belong to some caged wild animal. Dried blood trails from one nostril, remnants from a night spent chasing the moon. He looks like a shattered human being with a capacity for sudden violence, and my body naturally adjusts in anticipation of it.

His roar interrupts conversations all around us, and the guests start to draw closer to see what this new spectacle is. The porters are at the fringe of the crowd, ready to engage at the slightest request from me.

I spread my arms wide, amicably. "Well hullo, Darius. Have you been drinking again?"

"Fffuuck you. You're not him. HE DIED. Dead, dead, dead. Floating in a tub. I SAW IT. I ran. You're a ffake." He points at me, giving voice to my worst nightmare. But the crowd behind him isn't pointing towards me as they talk behind their hands, they're pointing at Darius. His reputation precedes him, and so far they don't take what this drunk says seriously. They continue to draw closer, ringing us tightly now.

When I speak next, I do it much louder, addressing the crowd like a showman. "Darius, be reasonable. Here I stand, myself in all my parts. Perhaps you've had a bit too much of the wine?"

As if I've struck a chord, he finds a new volume level in response. He stands straight, pointing at me, and screams. "HE'S AN IMPOSTER! A FAKE!" He looks around to see that he's drawn titters from the crowd, but they're still just focused on him, not what he's saying.

From my left side, Dotty interjects. "Darius, you're drunk and you're making more of a fool of yourself than usual. Go home, and for all our sake, get some help. You continue to not live up to your family name."

At this, he roars and swivels drunkenly to look at her. Her words seem to cut through and sober him. "You! You fucking cunt! You spread your legs for this *imposter* already?! You were Allen's girl, and you can't even tell this isn't him!" As he starts on his tirade, I motion to the porters behind him. They've been drawing slowly closer during this entire exchange.

"Remove this buff—" I start, but with a primal yell Darius rushes towards me. In his mind, this must be his heroic charge. The kind where he cannot lose, and everyone will later acknowledge his bravery. But his actions are telegraphed as if he's wearing a sign post. From the arching of his shoulder blade, I know that he'll punch with his right arm, and likely aim for my head. I don't feel fear, I just absorb the information methodically. The training I did with the combat drones kicks in nearly automatically, and as Darius throws his entire body behind a punch aimed at my face, I swivel deftly to the side.

In the training simulations, they suggest leaving a leg slightly outstretched during the pivot. If your timing is damn near perfect, or you're up against an unskilled opponent, they may trip on your extended leg and lose their balance. You can then take advantage of this loss of balance to turn the tide of the fight.

I'm a novice fighter, having only sparred with two drones for a few weeks, so I don't consider the consequences of Darius losing his balance. At least I tell myself that afterwards. Maybe I knew exactly what I was doing, or maybe Allen's ghost did. He strikes my leg with full force, the look on his face barely registering that his punch didn't land, and as he stumbles forward the energy he carried sends him careening into the railing on the balcony. It hits him right at his waist, and his momentum carries him forward. In an instant, he flips over the edge.

Shouts and gasps go up from the crowd, and time slows as I watch his feet perform a graceful arc through the air. Absurdly, I notice that his left shoe was untied, and as they rotate upwards I fixate on the flapping laces. I rush to try and grab his feet, but there is no speed where this is possible. Instead, I make it to the balcony to be the first one to see the remains of Darius sixty feet down, splattered across a poolside balcony beneath us. A woman in the pool screams, and as the small sound reaches us from far below, we can just see his blood slowly mix with the water.

I watch the patch of red slowly grow as the screams continue and multiply around me now. With a twist of shame I realize that I'm glad to see him dead, and I don't know if it's another echo of Allen's rage, or my own.

CHAPTER 8

After Darius fell, the party collapsed quickly. Most people went for the door immediately, but several stood around talking animatedly about what they saw. Eventually, our porters ushered them all out. Dotty stayed at my side until her father escorted her out. We had both known Darius before the drugs and the partying, and felt the weight of those memories. I stayed at the railing looking down for some time, part of me feeling the loss of a friend, and the other part relieved to be rid of him with such little effort. Eventually my father peeled me away, put a very tall glass of whiskey in my hand, and marched me back inside.

Three Inquisitors from the medical authority were there in minutes. I'd seen them once before from a distance, and thought they looked like a nightmare. Up close now, I'm sure they couldn't be the creation of a sane person. They all stand the same height, which towers above me, and are indistinguishable from each other. Their long, spindly arms extend past their knees and are capped with forearm-length, pointed fingers. Their faces are completely blank metal, and like they're pulled from some absurdist vision, they're all tailored in fitted suits and matching fedora hats. From the bottom of their trousers extend legs that nearly came to a point, but are capped in a small flat surface. For most things this would seem unstable. For them it did not.

The city didn't have much in the way of automatons, so the Inquisitors were a niche of their own, and they made everyone uncomfortable. As if designed to accentuate this discomfort, their joints could move in either direction, and as they talked they would slowly articulate them back and forth. Most that viewed it felt queasy, others fainted.

Two of the Inquisitors crawl down the exterior face of the building to gather the corpse, collect any evidence, and clean the surroundings. The third is left to question us. I stare at its hand, slowly folding in one direction, and then reversing and closing in the other. It's like a shimmering silver flower that continually blooms.

"Please, describe the events that led to the death of Darius Cloudspire."

I shudder at the clean, metallic voice. "Darius showed up to our party, I don't know when, and I don't know how much he had to drink or what he was on before he came here. It was evident that he was very drunk, and showed signs of using Luna—"

"Please, describe the evidence you saw of using the drug: Luna, and what showed his inebriation."

"His eyes were wild and bloodshot. There was puke on the front of his suit, I assumed his own. He had a blood trail from one nostril, and with his history that led me to believe he was on Luna—"

"But you did not directly confirm—"

"I did not directly confirm? Are you daft, machine? No, Darius showed up obviously fucked out of his mind, and then charged me and fell over the balcony!" My nerves are fried from the night, from the pressure of performing and the death. I know the Inquisitor's comment is meant to drive an emotional response, but anger raged through me all the same. My parents stare at me wide-eyed from the couch we all sit on, so I breathe out and settle back down.

The Inquisitor doesn't react at all to my outburst. There's no flinch, no step backwards. It never pauses in flexing its hand. *"Your aggression is noted. Please, why do you think Darius attacked you?"*

I realized the trap at this point, and nearly too late. These Inquisitors can certainly tell when a human was lying. If I don't tread carefully here I might wind up getting a DNA marker test tonight. *Wouldn't Darius have loved to know that.* "I believe he was angry that I had become a different person. Darius and I used to use Luna together, we were partners in that, but I overdosed and then I decided to change my life. I've been clean since then, and ignoring my old friends." *None of it was a lie. We'll see how it lands.*

The Inquisitor stares at me, unresponsive. I do not drop the blank gaze, but look around the face for clues of processing. In the silent room, I can hear the faint whirring and clicking of the automata brain that drives the hideous creation.

"Thank you for your honesty. Please, why did you throw Darius over the balcony?"

I know the question is meant to test my rage response, I know it damn well but I need to react as Allen would. I need to be the heir, angry at the slight from an inferior. And when I reach for his rage, it comes naturally. I immediately stand and thrust my face towards the machine's, so that I can see my reflection in its blank canvas as I scream. "You dare accuse me of purposefully killing an old friend?! On what grounds? Aren't you an evidence gathering robot? Look at the damn cameras then, you fucking pile of scrap! Darius didn't think about the balcony right behind me, I dodged the drunkard's punch and he tripped over my damn leg. In every other setting this would be a fucking comedy, not a tragedy."

I consider pushing the Inquisitor to add dramatic effect, my rage demands it, but I know that will not end well for me. Despite my parent's quiet entreaties behind me, I do not sit back down, but stay challenging it. They act surprised, but I know this reaction is expected from me. Even the Inquisitor might expect it.

"Again, your aggression is noted. These are standard interrogation tactics. I have conferred with the other Inquisitors, your claims are supported through the evidence. It has been decided that you are not at fault."

The Inquisitor stood taller, backed up a step, and in some sick parody, tipped its hat at us. Then it turned and walked out through the front door, its giant legs creating a slight tapping noise as they hit the wooden floor.

We never saw the other Inquisitors bring back the body, they must have scaled the building with it and gone directly to their tram outside.

I flopped back down on the couch, exhausted. My parents were both pale, and my mother cried quietly. As I sat back down, she put her arms around my neck and laid her head on my shoulder.

"You really must be careful with those machines, they can turn deadly if threatened. I was so afraid for you," she says as she cries into my jacket while my father mechanically rubs her back.

I couldn't sleep that night, and preferred to stay awake thinking than take a sleeping draught. False moonlight streamed in through the veranda, and created monsters in the shadows. I watched the patterns, and ran the events of the night over and over. When I closed my eyes, I saw Darius rotating over the balcony, I saw his shoe laces flapping through space as he plummeted. I've never killed someone, or been responsible for a death, and it's a weighty thing.

He was a fool, he charged me with the railing right behind me. Did he mean to push me over? That might have been me on the pavement below. I had to do what I did. Am I responsible? Did I know he'd go over the railing? Did I want him to die?

I'm staring out at the patio when it's suddenly blocked by a tram. I start to stand, my fatigued adrenaline response kicking in again, and then a pair of long legs carry someone out. In the moonlight, I recognize the silhouette immediately. The tram leaves, and I admire Dotty's beautiful form.

She reaches the door, and it unlocks silently with a biological key. *Of course she has one.* I'm quivering in anticipation, this is exactly what I need to happen tonight, but I still can't quiet a growing knot of shame. *Can I go through with this? There's no coming back from this, I'm lying to her and I'll have to keep lying to her until this is over. She'll hate me, she'll have every right to hate me. None of that matters, I need her to fall for me. It's a small evil, using her, compared to what I might achieve.* She steps into the room, and as I see her colored halfway in the light I lose all inhibition. There is only a sudden, overwhelming hunger.

I sit up in bed and throw my legs over the side, the covers barely hanging on between my legs. In the darkness we lock eyes, and I can see her hunger, as my own is rising. I hear Charon get up, and leave the room behind me, and then Dotty closes the distance. She straddles my lap and drives her mouth into mine.

We kiss hungrily, greedily, and when we separate I lift her dress over her head. Underneath are the beautiful curves I had seen hints of earlier, covered now in only beautiful lacy things. I traced them with my hands as I let her push me back against the bed. Her body feels strangely familiar under my hands, I already know where to stroke and where to grab. I'm hard against her thigh, and she rocks rhythmically against me.

In the Boroughs, there was none of this. I'd been with women before, but it was a dirty, exhausted type of love. Barely anyone had the energy for it, and no one had the money for dealing with pregnancy. This was an entirely different thing. This was hunger and passion and lust, we were burning brightly and reveling in it all. This was pleasure for the sake of it.

She stands up off me then, and I adjust backwards to bring my legs onto the bed. Without speaking, she takes off her lace unders and throws them across the room. There's one second where I get to admire her wrapped in moonlight, fully revealed and the most beautiful woman I've ever seen. She smiles, and sensuously crawls on the bed after me.

She grabs me, hard and throbbing in her hand, and as she put her legs on either side of me, she pushes me into her. Neither of us need to take things slow, and we buckle in the immediacy of the pleasure. She pushes me back against the bed then as she rocks her hips against me, sending waves of vibrating static through my body.

I trace my hands over every part of her as she grinds her pelvis against me, pressing harder by the second. Then I find her hips, and pull her down into me. Both of us moan with increasing ecstasy.

My eyes dart between her open, sensuous mouth and her softly bouncing breasts. Everything is immediate, everything is now, and together we become one bouncing, throbbing, rocking being. Memories of all my other nights with her coalesce into this one moment. There's a voyeurism in knowing they're not really mine.

"Oh yes, oh fuck, yes yes yes!" she screams as she pulsates violently against me, her back arching as her voice rises louder and louder. She starts contracting, and I explode inside her. All my muscles tighten, and I pull her onto me just as she grabs my ass and hip and pulls me into her. Nails dig into me, and the pain amplifies everything I feel until we both finish, exhausted.

With one last sigh, she flops down against me, both of us wet, dripping sweat, and panting. And I kiss her again, but sweeter now. And when our mouths part we stare into each other's eyes.

"I think I forgot to say hullo when I came in," she says, smiling as she curls into me. I chuckle, and pull her into me. Together, we find the sleep that was so elusive earlier.

I wake to the sound of the shower being used, I've slept late and I feel marvelously fresh. There's some pressure in me that's dissolved, and the world feels light and easy. I roll over and watch Dotty in the shower. It's halfway translucent and covered in steam so I can only make out some colored shapes moving. The shame I felt the night before is mostly quiet. I focus on the memory of enjoyment and the feeling of success. I'm making progress towards my goal by bringing her back to my side, I just need to not scare her away. Anyways, she's not interested in just Allen, she's interested in the thoughts I brought to him. *I don't need to feel shame for this, it's all worth it.*

There's a quiet knock at the door, and when I turn over to see what it is, the door cracks open enough for a breakfast cart to be pushed into the room and then shuts silently. It's a meal set for two. *I guess we weren't as discreet as she might have hoped last night, sound deadening only works so well.* I laugh quietly to myself, and getting out of bed pull on a thick purple robe embroidered with my initials to grab the cart by the door.

I'm pushing it over towards my bed when Dotty gets out of the shower. It dries her skin by blasting heated air on her as she exits, but she still wraps a towel around herself so quickly that I barely see anything. She locks eyes with me and freezes for a second, and then blushing looks away.

"Hey, Dotty, last night was unexpected, completely wonderful, but unexpected. I think for both of us. I hope you know I don't have any expectations about it. Honestly it was just great to be close to you again," I say, sitting down on the bed.

She walks over and sits next to me. "I really just came over to talk about Darius, and to talk about you, and how you've changed, and I just got overwhelmed when I came in," she says, looking away from me.

"Well then, let's set last night aside for now, and continue on that discussion while we eat. It seems at least our cooks were aware that I had a guest last night. They delivered this wonderful breakfast for two this morning." She smiles in profile at this. As it dries, her hair has taken on natural curls that I want to reach out and tussle, but I know it's not the right time.

"Okay, but turn around as I get dressed."

I oblige, laughing inwardly, and when I turn back later she's in last night's dress. I pull a tablecloth off the cart, and after spreading it on my mattress, set plates of food on it. We sit on either side like children, cross legged. The spread is marvelous. Fresh berries, real eggs, and fluffy thin cakes that are browned perfectly on either side and coated in butter.

"How are you feeling about Darius?" she asks, after we've both taken a few silent bites of food.

"We lost Darius a long time ago, just like I was lost for a while. I don't know if he would've ever come back though. Last night, it was horrible, but as I thought about potential ways Darius could have gone, well it wasn't the worst thing I could think of. He didn't take anyone else with him." She nods at this while looking down.

She raises her gaze and meets mine. "Why do you think he was convinced you were an imposter? I know his mind was probably shattered, but he seemed so fixated on it."

I've got to tread lightly here. I consciously avoid squirming under the pressure, I know that will be a tell. "When I overdosed, Darius was with me. He left me to die, probably afraid of any consequences. Thankfully, I was found by a couple of Sickos before I was too far gone. Darius must have been convinced that I died there."

There are tears falling down her face now. "So you really did—" She makes a small choked noise, seems to settle herself, and then continues, "You really did almost die from Luna?"

I nod my head solemnly in affirmation. I've never been someone that could lie well, there was never a reason for it in the Boroughs. The weight of the truth is starting to twist my guts. There's a thing growing in me that wants to just tell her the whole story, to come clean and let things fall how they will. I check it. I have to live this lie.

"The Sickos took me to the only hospital they knew, a place where they spend time recovering. They couldn't unlock my screen to see who I am, and I certainly wasn't in a place to tell them. I spent the next few weeks in the hospital fading in and out of consciousness. When I finally woke up, I was surrounded by people wrecked from disease transfer. *The Box*, as they call it down there. It was shameful to see all these people barely existing, having to choose sickness to live, while I'd nearly died from living too excessively." Even though the story is fake, real emotions are flooding me. I can see the scene, and the weight of Allen's memories makes me feel real shame about it. Dotty reaches out and runs her hand through my hair, sweeping it back behind my ear.

"I'm glad that you didn't die there. And I'm so glad that you're choosing to change your life. Sometimes, we get lucky enough to have the opportunity to learn from mistakes, but it's still hard to choose to." There's a look in her eyes that I can't place.

I nod and wipe my face. "If you'd like, I want to take you there. To the hospital. It's a dreadful place, but also where I learned what it's like for those down in the Boroughs."

She smiles and nods, with tears in her eyes. "Okay, sure, I want to see it. But can we also just spend some time together being happy? I'm not a morose person, and I want to focus on this." She squeezes my hand as she says it, and a happy warmth floods me.

Flashing a brilliant smile I say, "That sounds wonderful to me."

CHAPTER 9

After Dorothy leaves that morning, I send a wax-sealed letter to Brian stamped with the ring of Allen Cloudspire. I could have tried to find a covert way of sending a message, but if it had been found out the optics would be worse. Still, I have to assume that it might be read by the wrong person, so I can only be cryptic in my message.

Sir Brian,

I am planning to come visit your hospital with a friend to show her where I spent my recovery. We will be there tomorrow, around midday. I hope we shall not be a nuisance, and that you will be there to tell her about my time with you.

Your friend,
Allen Cloudspire

I stare at the letter for some time, but I think adding anything more will sound conspicuous. I seal it and hand it to our staff letter courier with instructions that it must be delivered immediately. I can only hope that Brian will see the threads of the story I'm creating and help me to weave them together.

Dotty joins me at the house the next morning for breakfast, and when we're done I call Joe for a ride down to Meadow Hearth. There's a faint smile on his lips when he sees her next to me on our landing pad. Without a word he opens the door to the tram for us, and as I'm climbing in after Dotty he pats me on the back and gives me a wink. He walks back to the pilot's cabin, and we expertly lift off to join the swirling arc of trams around Cloud Spire.

"Down to the city for the day, Sir Allen? Shall I wait around for you, or come back later?"

"We'll send word later on, Joe. Dotty's taking me out for a nice dinner." I see a smile flash across Joe's face in profile, and I notice then that there's a teenage girl in the front with him.

"Oh hullo Josephine, I didn't know you would be joining us today."

As if she's been waiting for me to notice, she quickly spins around in her seat, sending her blonde pigtails bouncing, and gives me a massive smile. "Hullo Sir Allen, I'm so happy to see you again! When my da told me that you were back, oh I was just so puffed. And oh wow, your eyes! What a marvel they are sir, I'm certain they must be the talk of the town. And hullo to you too, you must be Dorothy Sungate. I've heard oh so much about you and you really are more beautiful in person—"

Joe reaches across and pats her on the leg. "Calm down dear, remember as a driver we should speak *very little* unless they ask us questions. Beg your pardon, Sir Allen, I'm taking little Joe here out for some lessons today and she was so eager to get to see you again."

Josephine flashes me a smile, and flips around again in her seat. I laugh deeply. "No problem at all Joe." I reach up and ruffle Josephine's hair from behind. "It's good to see you again too, munchkin."

Dotty watches the interaction quietly. There's something on her mind, I wonder if she never saw Allen interact with Joe and his daughter before.

As our conversation fades, Joe toggles on the transparency and I stare down at the city. We race over the top of Sky's Reach. Towering structures pass beneath us so close that it feels like my dangling feet might catch on them. As we get closer to Meadow Hearth, the ground races up and the lives down there become more clear. After my short stint in the clouds, everything here looks dirtier and dimmer than I remember. Cheap lights line the front of shops and poverty ravaged people litter the walks. I can see the way clothes hang from their frail bodies as we're coming up to our landing pad, and I can feel the same sensation inside my own clothes, inside my own body. It's a memory from a different life.

Suddenly we've landed, and Joe is throwing open the door and giving Dotty a hand as she exits. The pad is right next to Brian's hospital, and I stare at the once familiar building as I leave the tram behind. The structure used to look so tall and imposing, it's the only three story building for blocks. Now it looks like a broken, squat hovel. The paint is faded and dirty—what was once a proudly white building I see now as a dingy gray. Several windows are broken out and boarded over with metal sheeting, and the unbroken ones have bars across them to prevent people stealing medical equipment. There's a neon light outside that's flashing intermittently that simply reads *Hospital*.

Sickos line the walk leading up to the building, some of them are leaving in better health and some of them hover around the entrance like flies, trying to make the decision if they need to pay for a hospital this time. I know the weights of that scale too well. I recognize a few of them and start to hide my face, before I remember there's no need. In the corner next to the stairs leading to the main entrance, someone's curled up in a pile of rags, either sleeping or dead.

"Are you sure you're okay here, sir?" Joe asks, looking around with a worried expression on his face. Dotty looks to me as well, obviously wondering a similar thing.

"We'll be fine, Joe. These people are hurting, not looking to hurt."

Joe nods once and climbs back into the tram. It lifts off behind us silently, and we're left in the thick of it. A few people on the walk glance in our direction, but we're so far separated from their world that they quickly move on. I reach out and grab Dotty's hand, and we walk into the hospital.

The overwhelming smell of cheap disinfectant nearly knocks us over when I open the door. It brings back so many memories inside me, and for a moment I'm lost in them until a familiar man walks out of the door to the ward.

He bows comically deeply. "*Monsieur* Allen, I am so pleased to see you again."

Inside myself, I'm ecstatic and laughing. I know he's poking fun at me, and I just want to hug the bastard. Instead I walk up and grab his outstretched hand in a forearm handshake. He's surprised at first, but takes it in stride. "Well met, Brian. I am glad to see you again."

He turns to Dorothy next and bows deeply again. "I'm pleased to meet you, my lady." He offers his hand to her.

She shakes it heartily. "Dorothy Sungate, a pleasure to meet you, Doctor."

"Please, I only get to be a doctor on my best days. Usually I just patch these idiots back together," he says, pointing a thumb behind him towards the ward. Then, reconsidering, he adds, "Sorry for my language, ma'am, we speak differently down here than in Sun Gate, I'm sure."

This tickles Dotty, and she laughs deeply. "Trust me Brian, you don't offend. Please, speak however you're comfortable."

Brian nods, and as if he's just remembered something, rummages through the pockets of his white lab coat. He pulls out two circular, metallic discs the size of his palm, and hands one to each of us. I turn it over in my hand, the only remarkable feature is a small, thumb-sized rubber button on one face.

"Those are personal infection shields. They make a terrible racket while they're active, and only last for an hour or so, so we barely use them here, but they'll prevent almost anything from reaching you. I'm sure you both have a stellar immune system, but I really can't stand the idea of you catching something from my hospital."

Dotty flips the thing over in her hand, she's never seen one either. "I'm surprised we don't see these in Sun Gate more. What will keep you safe, Brian?"

"Oh miss, thank you for the concern. This is my daily existence, I trust in simple tools." At this he brandishes a small cloth mask and shows how it fits over his mouth and nose. "As for why you don't see them more, well you'll understand when you use it."

At this, Brian pulls his mask on, and indicates we follow him. We approach the automatic steel door that leads to the hospital ward, and it slides noiselessly open. Having been here before, I know that it uses a sophisticated bio-lock, and will only open in the presence of Brian or his staff. Dotty and I take out our shields, and shrugging at each other, we both press the buttons simultaneously.

We both watch each other as a translucent covering emanates from the shield, and wraps around our bodies. It's a fast process, and in the end Dotty's face is completely blurred out, but I find that my vision is unaffected. A terrible, high-pitched whine seems to resonate inside of the shield. It's piercing enough that the thought of spending an hour with it makes me nauseous. And then the itching starts, like my entire body is being shocked by waves of static electricity, and as I watch Dotty I see from her body language that she's in the same discomfort.

"Brian, is the itching normal?" I ask, as we walk into the ward.

He turns back to us and gives a huge smile. "Ah yes, there is that. The price of safety my friends!"

We quickly forget the whining and itching as the sights of the ward take us over. The hallway has doors on either side, and most of them are open. Patients sit inside in a variety of conditions, some unconscious with oxygen, some writhing unpleasantly in pain, and some just sleeping soundlessly. On each door there's a board, and in erasable ink the affliction is written. We see children with cases of pneumonia, laboring to breathe under oxygen masks, and as the age increases so does the severity of diseases. The number of cancer patients my age brings tears to my eyes. They've taken the big gamble and most of them won't win that bet. Dorothy pauses at several of the doors, silent and looking in—with the shield active I can't tell her reaction.

Several doors we pass are closed, with nothing written on the board. I know what's behind them, but I wait for her to ask the question.

"Brian, most of these doors are open with diseases labeled. What's behind the closed doors then?" she asks, meekly.

"Ahh miss, well those are patients that are too far gone for knowing the affliction to be any good. For them, we just keep them comfortable, and monitor the progress. For a lot of the people in those rooms, we'll be the last people to see them off. There's no one else to do it, so we try to be with them at the end." He pauses, reflecting. "Sir Allen here had his door closed for the first week, we didn't think his liver would recover. But he's stronger than most I'd wager."

Dotty's head whips to stare at me, and even with the shield I can tell this news has hit her hard. I'm silently ecstatic that Brian has given credibility to my story, this was the big wager in coming here, but in the same instant I'm pierced by a hot stab of shame. *I'm so sorry, Dotty. I know this is a terrible thing to do.*

I have to create this lie, I need you to believe, I need you to trust me. It's for a greater good.

We keep walking, and at the end of the hall, we turn into an empty room. It's clean and sterile, and after a moment I recognize it. This is the same room I woke up in, months ago. This is where Nicholas did almost die. I stare into the same mirror that showed my wasted body then, and now it just shows me a blurred human shape. Some combination of parts and people exist behind this shield, and I'm just as confused about it as the mirror is.

"This was Allen's room. It was empty when I got his message so I thought I might show it on the tour." Brian motions around the room.

Dotty is frozen in the doorway, and after a moment says, "I'm going to be ill."

Brian nods, and goes into action. He ushers her down the hall quickly and shows her the bathroom. When he comes back, we're alone for a few moments.

"This is a damn terrible thing you're doing, son," he whispers.

"I know, Brian, I know. She doesn't deserve this, but the end justifies these means. She's the best bet I have for gaining access to Sun Gate, I need her if I want to shut all this down."

He reaches out and grabs my shoulder. "Remember, don't lose your humanity in this. The end doesn't always justify the means, you can lose yourself down that path. There's real people you'll hurt, and it will make any success hollow."

I want to protest, to argue the point with him. I want to convince him that I'm still the person he knows, but we hear the bathroom door open again, and Brian takes his hand off of my shoulder.

Dotty comes back to the room, but won't come past the doorway. "Allen, I've seen enough. How about we get some fresh air now?"

"Of course." We walk quickly back out of the ward, and turn off our shields. I can see now what the experience has done to her. Her dark skin has turned ashen, and her eyes are red-rimmed from crying. I try to give my shield back to Brian, but he holds up his hands.

"Please, keep those trinkets. I never use them, and we don't get enough visitors to need them."

"Thanks for your time, Brian. It is good to see you again." I want desperately to hug him, to spend time here talking like I used to. I hadn't realized how much I'd missed him, one of the last vestiges of my old life, until this moment.

He smiles, and the pain in his face says the same thing. "It's good to see you too, Allen. And wonderful to make your acquaintance, Miss. It's very heart-warming to see such compassion from someone of your standing." He bows again, but there is no mockery in it this time. "Please, take care of yourselves."

We turn and exit the building, and I put my arm around Dorothy. For a few minutes we stand in the field across from the hospital, and she cries into my shoulder. I feel wretched watching her.

"Those people, those children, what sort of existence is that?"

"I know. It seemed so abstract to me before, but when I saw them suffering...it changed me."

At this she hugs me, hard. And despite how awful the lying feels, I love her touch. For a second, I let the story be real in my mind. I let it all be true, I let myself be the prodigal son returned, and damn I just wish I could hold onto the sweetness of it all. I wish I never had to tell her that it was a lie, it was all a deception. *I'm so fucking sorry Dorothy Sungate, I will never be able to atone for this.*

We hail a public tram and travel across the ring of Meadow Hearth to the Metal Oyster. The music club and restaurant is one of the oldest stalwarts of the city, and it's one of the only melting pots where you'll see people from every level. At the bar on the lower level, you'll find Meadow Hearth locals drowning themselves after their shift work. Mechanics rub elbows with school teachers and line cooks, all ready to forget it all for a few hours. The upper two levels are dedicated to dining, you'll see parties of people from Sky's Reach executing business deals, Cloud Spire magnates boozing on fancy champagne, and the occasional Sun Gate ordering a plate of pricelessly rare food. And in the shadowy corners are all the Sickos, making deals with people from every other rung.

The outside of the building is non-descript, a three story concrete shell without windows and a pulsing neon sign that shows a clam opening and closing. No one remembers what the name means, or why the sign shows the wrong mollusk—it's a place as old as the city itself. The inside is low-lit, plush red velvet wraps the antique wood surfaces. There's a staircase on either side that goes to the upper levels, but the center of them is left open and ringed by a balustrade, so everyone can stare down.

At the center of this whole mess is a stage, and there's nothing else like it in the city. Some nights, musicians play the stage, and on others there are dancers, or storytellers, and the whole thing slowly spins. It feels other-worldly to watch, and everyone seems to have a story of the life changing experiences they've had here. Tonight there's a lone player at an electric keyboard. His music morphs and twists with successive looping tracks so that if I close my eyes, it sounds like a three piece jazz band.

The house-waiter recognizes Dorothy immediately and we're sat on the upper floor in one of the best seats, right next to the balcony so we can stare down onto the stage. I've made a few deals here over the years, but never sat down for a meal. We order the kitchen specialty, a roasted white fish served with delicious small potatoes, carrots, and slices of lemon. One of the biggest mysteries of the Metal Oyster is where their food supply comes from. Nowhere else in the city serves fish. It's a tightly guarded secret that adds to the magic.

"What do you think?" Dorothy asks after we've both taken our first bite.

The succulent fish dances flavor around my mouth, the salt and soft texture meld with the lemon and char from roasting. It's beautiful. I try not to let her see that it's one of the best things I've ever tasted, but all I want to do is close my eyes and savor it.

"It's magnificent," I get out after swallowing.

She laughs. "I know, I love it here. It's nice to come here with you, in the past you never wanted to leave the high rises. What did you used to say? *It's too dirty down there,*" she says mockingly, and smiles.

I smile back. "Well, as it turns out I was very mistaken. If it's dirty down here then I'd like to play in it." I spear a potato and pop the crusted morsel into my mouth.

"How do you think we get the rest of the city to see the beauty and culture down here?"

I scoff. "They have to value the people first, I think."

At this she nods, and looks around the room. Her eyes drift over to a table that I've been watching since we sat down. They're half shrouded in darkness, but you can just make out someone eating a very nice meal with an emaciated person sitting across from them. They're having an animated discussion and pointing to a sheet of paper that sits between them.

"That's a Sicko isn't it, over there making a deal?"

"Yes," I say, my face clouding over.

"It's strange, do you think they make all their deals in places like this?"

I think back to my own time, sitting in a dimly lit booth across from the richest man I'd ever met. He was sporadically crippled by coughing fits. "Only the big ones, I bet."

She blanches at this, probably realizing we're watching as someone's last job is being written. They both stand and shake hands. The person that was eating leaves the shadows, she's a tall brunette in a stunning black dress. Most people would think she was the picture of health, but I pick up on the subtle sallow color under her make-up, the bags under her eyes, and the too tight of skin. *Some cancer, I'd bet.*

Dorothy snaps her eyes away before the woman sees us. "That's Patricia Sungate, I've known her since we were children," she whispers to me.

I nod, still looking at the Sicko who has sat back down at the table, his head in his hands.

Without a second thought, I motion to a waiter and ask him to bring me a second plate. Dorothy watches as I portion off a chunk of fish, and pile the plate with vegetables. I hand it to the waiter and point to the man. "Tell him we ordered too much and hope that he enjoys this meal." The waiter's eyes widen, but he obliges. When the man turns around to stare at us, his mouth gaping, I curtly nod to him and look away.

Dotty looks at me questioningly. "Why'd you do that?" She's obviously not mad, but seems to have never considered sharing her plate with someone else.

"In my time at the hospital, I learned that the Boroughs are a culture of sharing. They support those around them when they have excess, and ask for help when they're in need. We have an almost unlimited capacity to share with these people. It just seemed right, I guess."

A fire builds in her eyes, something has inspired her. "But Allen, that's it! I've been so focused on trying to change things politically, I've never even thought to try at the ground level. We can easily set up a moving kitchen in the Boroughs and cook for them! Maybe we can show others to value the people down here, too."

My heart swells at the idea of bringing food back to the people I love, and tears come to my eyes. "Okay, let's do it! I know a place that we can start, one of the Sickos from the hospital showed me his home in the Boroughs before he passed." My mind is rushing through how this might go. I know it will be risky, but I can't turn away from the possibility.

We chat through details for the rest of our meal, and both of us are lifted up by the planning, excited to see what impact we can have. Tomorrow, we'll go to my family home. There's a love growing in my chest for this woman, and I'm excited to take her there, even if she won't know it. I wish I could introduce her to my mother, I wish I could tell her everything true and have her not hate me. The sweetness of the thought is intoxicating.

As we're leaving, the man I gave food to is crying silently over his plate. He's only taken a few bites, and I'm sure is saving the rest to share with his family. It's what I expected to see.

Chapter 10

The next morning is a flurry of activity. My father is disinterested in joining, but my mother's eyes light up at the idea. When I tell the cooks, porters, and waiters our plan, the appreciation in the air is palpable. As much as they live in our world, they still have family and friends down there. I ask Joe for transportation, and he finds us a tram with a massive box in the back instead of passenger seating. It's rough around the edges, and meant for moving furniture or large pieces of equipment, but for tonight it's perfect. Dotty enlists two others from Sun Gate, Priscilla and Archibald—they're not exactly her friends so much as people prone to gossip.

The cooks spend the day roasting twenty chickens and making gallons of soup and rice. To everyone from the higher levels, this would be a very bland, boring meal. But I know it will be the first time for many to taste real food, for many of them this will be a night they remember for the rest of their lives. News of it will spread across the Boroughs.

By late afternoon all the preparations are made, and everyone is busy loading things into the tram. My porters are surprised to see Dotty and I helping them, but they don't protest. Dotty and I cram into the front seat with Joe. It's immediately a different relationship than when we're being driven around. We're part of the work now, and I can see from the look on her face that Dotty is loving all of it. I feel more like myself than I have in weeks.

People are just starting to return from work when we park in the middle of a poorly lit street in the Boroughs. The first thing out are the lights. We string out lamps and power them using the tram's energy. From darkness, the street blazes to life, and I can see curious faces looking out windows already. We rush out the folding tables we borrowed from a local shop, tablecloths are thrown down, and as the cooks are starting to set up warmers and plates I see young Anna Fiveboroughs creeping closer to get a look.

I grab a sliver of chicken, and kneel down and beckon to her. She comes over hesitantly, and I hand her the morsel.

"Tell everyone you know that we're going to share food here, real food. There's no cost, we just want to give what we have. If they don't believe you, show them this piece of chicken. If you don't eat it and come back with it, I'll give you two more." Her eyes have grown so wide they look like they might pop out. She looks from the chicken, to my eyes, and then back to the food. And then she grabs it and runs off, and I laugh heartily.

By the time we have a rough serving area set up, there's already a line forming. I can tell people are hesitant, but interested to see what happens here. Everyone that came with us gets a job,

Dotty and my mother are at one end serving chicken, and I'm at the very end to dollop soup on top of everything. And then we turn it all on and the chaos begins.

People laid low by life stream through the line, and I can see the gratitude in their eyes as I put soup into their bowl. They realize that this food is theirs, that I am not going to take it back from them. Emotions are high all down the street, there are tears and sudden shouts of jubilation. As I run out of soup, Archibald and Priscilla bring me stock pots of more—they're helping the porters refill food stations all down the line. I'm certain they've never done work like this, and the discomfort is clear on their faces. We feed an endless stream of people, and it seems the more we feed the longer the line grows. I can feel word spreading all through the Boroughs, there's an excitement in the air that I've never seen down here.

I know this has all been a success when the dancing starts. It's something I've only seen on a few celebrations here, but fast feet come with full bellies and light hearts. The singing starts slowly, and as it builds a circle for dancing forms. Soon it's full of couples, the young, the old, and the sick. I look over to Dotty and we lock eyes, there's so much satisfaction in her face that it makes my heart hurt.

I look up to serve soup to the next person in line, and lock eyes with Nicholas's mother. With my mother. She's been moving mechanically through the line, her eyes barely fluttering up to the people serving food, so I didn't notice her. Her bowl slips from her grasp, and my hand shoots out to grab it and steady it.

"But, how?" The words escape her in a barely audible whisper.

From my peripheral I can tell that no one is paying attention to us yet, and there's no one in earshot as long as we keep our voices quiet.

"Ma, it's me. I'm fine, ma. I'm going to bring the system down. They don't know," I whisper this in a rush, and her eyes grow wider. She's crying, and I'm crying.

"Nicholas." It's all she can get out, choking back sobs.

I can tell that Dotty is starting to pay attention, so I whisper, "I love you ma. I'm fine. Please keep moving, don't make a fuss here or they'll notice."

This sinks in immediately and it's clear she understands. A massive grin splits her face, and I pour soup into her bowl. Through teary eyes, she winks at me, and leaves.

We continue to serve people until we run out of food. There's so many more here than I anticipated, news must have spread across half of the Boroughs. When we run out, those with food still in their bowls share it with those who didn't get any.

Putting everything away is light work. I hadn't been paying attention, but several of the locals were helping Priscilla and Archibald clean things as we emptied them. Those two look exhausted, but there's a new pride in their eyes as they look around to everyone they helped. We take everything down, and everyone on the street chips in to move it back into the tram. Both Dorothy and I are exhausted when we pile back in with Joe—she falls asleep on my shoulder, and even though I try to resist it, I fall asleep on Joe's. He wakes us when we land in Cloud Spire like a kind father, and we drowsily move towards the house.

On my way there Joe stops me, and with the kindest smile and a tear in his eye he reaches out to rest a hand on my shoulder. "I knew you were a good man, Sir Allen, but tonight—thank you for what you've done." He nods at that and leaves.

That night, I slept with Dotty again. It wasn't the fire and lust of the first time, but full of that same slow sweetness that's crept into my chest. Watching her through this past night, her joy and graciousness at sharing with my people, it's split me wide open. She looked at me differently too, with less irony and more contemplative quiet. Contentedness. Our bodies found a natural rhythm together, and we moved with it. Clothes came off gradually, and we rolled around the bed. Sometimes she was on top, sometimes I was. We blurred together, and savored each moment. Our rhythm built and built, a tidal wave coming into the coast to consume everything, until we crashed down together, spent.

Afterwards, we held each other and talked about the night. There's an excitement there, a natural passion. She slowly stroked my chest, and I played with her hair, our minds else-where.

"Who was that old woman that was talking to you, at the end of the night?" she asks, suddenly seeming to remember.

"Someone that was very grateful to see me. Her son died in the hospital while I was there, and she remembered my face."

Dotty nods in contemplation of that.

"Did you see Priscilla and Archibald cleaning? I wonder if they've ever done that a day in their lives." We chuckle together.

"There was so much tonight that was lovely and new," Dotty says contemplatively. I think she means our moving feast, but part of me also thinks she's speaking about me, and my heart swells with pride. "I want you to come with me to Sun Gate tomorrow. I know you've never been, but I want you to see what it's like. We have a long way to go to change things," she says, her voice trailing off.

She's falling asleep, and I pull her tighter to me. Nestled together, we drift off.

When I traveled to Cloud Spire for the first time, I remember being in awe of the luxury and riches. It was so far beyond Five Boroughs, so much wealthier, that it was a completely different way of existing. I naively thought that Sun Gate would be more of the same, everything a bit nicer, the ceilings higher and more money everywhere. Like Cloud Spire, but amplified.

Instead, Sun Gate makes Cloud Spire look like it's from a different age. Where Cloud Spire shocked me with its luxury, Sun Gate makes everything else look backward with its technology. I'm let through the gates after Dotty signs multiple copies of holographic paperwork, her finger swishing through the air over the documents. It's a small thing to them, commonplace, but I've never seen technology like it. The guards inject a time-sensitive bio-chip into my left arm, tell me if I don't leave before the time runs out it will kill me, and open the doors.

"Nice welco—" I start to say, but trail off as I see what's on the other side. All I can do is gape at what I find on the other side.

People fly around me, seemingly headed in every direction. On their backs are mesh wings with glistening purple nodes. Some of them are more ornate than others, with diamond be-jeweled edges. They shimmer and sparkle as they soar through the air in a flashing dazzle of beauty. I trace the arcs of the fliers until I start to grow dizzy.

Beneath them, there are cherry trees planted along the walk, and I watch as the occasional passerby picks a handful to pop in their mouth. Underneath it are the bleeding remains of cherries crushed by passing feet. There's such a bizarre callousness here in the casual waste of so much food, and the obliviousness of everyone to it.

There are robots everywhere, in all shapes and sizes. They clean the walk, water plants, and sell food on the street corner. Some of them are shaped to resemble humans, and others are shaped to their task. For several seconds, I watch a flat disc scurry around the pavement, eating up discarded trash as it deftly avoids footfalls from the passersby. I'd always thought Inquisitors were the only automata in the city.

It strikes me now what I'm up against to infiltrate this place. There's not just an immense amount of money here, not just the center of the city's security network. Sun Gate has a level of technology that is generations beyond the rest of the city. For the first time, I'm struck with a certainty of how little I actually understand of our world.

"Close your mouth, or they'll throw you back through the gates," Dotty whispers in my ear playfully as she squeezes my bicep. I clamp it shut, but keep looking around with wild eyes. I'm resistant, but she steers me into the fray.

As we walk down the path, I notice the Inquisitors. They're perched everywhere, some of them lean against the sides of doorways, some of them hang from trellises. Wherever I look, they're there in the background, observing. Dorothy notices my eyes darting around.

"Good, you noticed them. With great wealth comes great surveillance, I guess. You stop seeing them after a time, which might be even more concerning. Just be happy it's them and not the Centurions on the street," she shudders slightly at the thought. It's the second time I've heard of these guards, and I wonder what sort of beast they are to make the Inquisitors preferable.

The walk splits off into a nature park. Even small plants are rare in the lower levels, so this is totally new to me. Trees line the grassy, rolling hill in front of me. There are a few benches and gazebos sprinkled around, and people lounge on the grass in seemingly total peace. They read books, chase children, and eat from small baskets of food. It's a wholesome and pure sight that radiates innocence in its simplicity. I can't imagine the money to achieve it.

A robot in a suit meets us on the walk, and holds out a suitcase towards Dotty. It's built like an Inquisitor, but stands at the same height as me instead of looming over us both. It has the same blank metal face that defies understanding.

"Allen, meet Sophia. They manage our house. Since few people from other districts are allowed into Sun Gate, most of the families here rely on their kind to keep things in order. She's named after an old caretaker of mine, a young woman from Meadow Hearth."

I bow slightly to Sophia in greeting, and they respond similarly.

Dotty reaches forward and opens the suitcase that the robot holds out to her. She reaches in and takes out two pairs of shimmering purple wings. They're smaller here. When not expanded into their mesh shapes they fit in the palm of a hand. It's enough that I can tell where this is heading though. My stomach drops.

"Dotty, I don't know how to—"

"Well of course you don't know how to, don't worry. Yours will be in guide mode, they'll follow me the entire time. You'll be completely fine." She gives me an assuaging smile, and squeezes my arm again. Then she grabs one pair of wings, and puts it to the center of my back, right below my neck. Ice spreads across my shoulder blades and a new awareness grows in me. *I can feel them like they're a part of me.* "It's only uncomfortable the first time, you get used to it pretty quick."

I watch as she attaches her own at the base of her slender neck. Green tendrils shoot out on contact, like ivy growing across her bronze skin, they snake across her shoulder blades and down her spine.

"These attach organically to your spine's motor control nerves, so once you learn how to use them, it's no different than a new pair of legs."

She grabs my hand, and together we lift off the ground. For a second my legs kick around, searching for solid ground, but with focus I still them. For a few moments we hover there, ten feet off the ground. She drops my hand and I'm certain I'm going to fall, but I don't. I just float there, next to her.

"Okay, we're going to meet some politicals for lunch. I wanted you to see how everything works up here, I didn't know if you'd believe me if I tried to just tell you." At this she turns and we fly into the air. I'm suspended several feet behind her, but despite the rushing air I can hear her voice perfectly. It seems to resonate through my bones. *The wings must have some sort of communication function.*

"There are two main political parties here, but don't let that trick you into thinking they're that different. You heard my father call me a neo-prog the other night, that's slang for *progressive*. I'm not one but I certainly align closer to their ideas. They're pushing for more opportunities for the lower quadrants, more technology dissemination, but only so far as it doesn't affect their own power. The other is the *classical* party, although those on the outside just call them colonialists. They're pleased with the current state, and only want changes to make the lower quadrants more directly subservient. They are by far the majority. They both believe they're on top of this society due to their own merit, not some luck of birth, and that makes them inherently better than those lower. There is no empathy here, so don't try to find it. It's imperative you understand that."

I'm listening, but it's hard to completely absorb what she's saying. As she talks, we're flying around buildings, dodging jutting verandas and people heading in other directions. She does it all naturally, without thinking, and as it's happening I start to learn how. Through my wings, I sense the upcoming obstacles like I have a pair of outstretched, invisible hands. I can feel the people flying into our path, and it seems only natural to move out of their way. The world rushing by is shimmering and golden, and I realize that it's also moving. The buildings are constantly swaying as if in some invisible wind. They look alive, like the trees in the park.

"No one here, or at least no formed political party, seems to champion that our society is unjust. That we abuse those on the lower levels, and use them to maintain a lifestyle that should be impossible. The very idea of that makes most people uncomfortable, or worse. It threatens their way of life, and nothing could be more heretical in Sun Gate than that."

She pauses here for some time, so I look around to the surroundings that are rushing by. Parks dot the landscape up here. Smaller towers, that still dwarf those in Cloud Spire, ring the central tower in regular intervals. We dart through their massive, swaying forms. From up above, they must look like a sea of golden grass.

Noticing my stares, Dotty says, "The towers sway as a signal of the energy production of the city. When we're in a surplus, they move like this. From what I've heard, they've always moved. You may not know this, but our city harvests energy from the outside environment."

The outside environment? It's a thought that I've never really dwelled on. There's only ever been the city. I'm about to ask more when my attention is drawn elsewhere.

We're close enough now that my vision is pulled into the immensity of the central tower, the medical research facility. I bend and crane my neck to see the peak, and find that it blends seamlessly with the top of the city. One central, golden pillar that stretches the entire height. Unlike the other buildings, it does not sway. There are no verandas on it. Its surface is pure, unapproachable and solemn in the landscape of seemingly organic structures that surround it. *How am I going to get in there?*

"We're meeting three politicals today, it's not important that you know their names. They certainly won't remember yours. They're leaders of the progressives, but be careful what you say all the same. They're dangerous, all of them."

We barrel over the edge of a veranda, so close that the railing almost smashes my knees, and then quickly slow and float down to it. As we land our wings shrink down again and curl around the base of our necks. As I watch Dotty from behind, the wings camouflage into her skin and disappear from sight. I smooth the tuxedo that Dotty picked out this morning, and follow her across the balcony. I act as if it's the most natural thing for me to rocket through an unknown, highly advanced city with technology that's totally new to me, to land on a veranda where people sit calmly reading and sipping coffees at tiny tables. My legs are shaking, but I tighten all my muscles to keep it from being visible.

I follow her to a pair of luxurious couches that face each other, a small marble table between them is scattered with coffees and pastries. Two men and a woman lounge on one couch, and are deep in conversation as we approach. One is the fattest man I've seen in the city, his massive belly seems barely contained by his waistcoat. He has a giant mustache and ruddy, red cheeks. The other seems his mirror opposite, rail thin and pale, he sits on the opposite end unsmiling. The other is the picture of feminine power, in a wonderfully fitted pantsuit and trendy purple fedora. She sees us approach and stands, giving Dotty a shark's smile.

"Oh hullo darling, I see you brought a *friend* with you as well. How delicious," the woman says, her predatory grin deepening. I nearly expect to see her teeth sharpened to points.

"Allen Cloudspire" I say, bowing towards them.

"Yes, yes. Please sit down." She motions towards the adjacent couch, spurning my introduction.

"Dorothy, you mentioned that there was some legislation that you wished to introduce at the council?" the thin pale man says.

"Yes, thank you three for your time today. I've spent some time in the lower levels recently, and what I saw shocked me. We need to propose a moratorium on the selling of terminal illnesses and—"

"A what?! And how do you expect us to sell that dung heap?" the rotund man interjects.

Dotty is thrown on her back foot, so I interject. "Life expectancies in the Boroughs are near thirty five years of age. This has forced the average age for parenting to be around fifteen years old to keep population numbers from declining.

"Oh he's adorable, *and* he has ideas. Dorothy, you must let me borrow him for an evening," the woman says, flashing her shark smile again. I barely suppress a shudder. Seeing Dorothy's face sour, she adds, "Oh I'm only mostly kidding, dear, no need to fuss."

"While I'm sure that presents a noteworthy long-term issue for stock numbers—" the thin man starts.

Now it's Dorothy's turn. "*Stock numbers?!* Are you a colonialist now, Percival? I'm talking about basic humanity here, we're killing them off while those in Sun Gate live well over a century." The thin man blanches at the reproach. "They are not cattle for us to use, no matter what those assholes in the council believe."

"Oh leave Percival alone, you know what he means. The messaging here is horrible, it would tank our ratings. We don't all share your sense of martyrdom, dear."

"She's right, Dorothy. You know we can't afford that. Why, we've just been making some great gains in our decency campaign. Our polling suggests that the kindness towards those in the lower levels has increased by double digits!" Mustache adds.

I can't help myself. "Asking a wolf to be decent while it's currently eating a lamb sounds like an approach that disregards what the lamb wants entirely."

He rounds on me, his face turning red. "And what would you know about it, boy?"

A smarter man than me would have realized this is the point to shut up. *I did not come this far to be quiet at the table of these monsters.* "I lived down there for a month, I saw their lives. They are stuck in a trap where they have to bargain their lives to eat, but the bargain kills them. Imagine that you were born into that—"

The mustached man suddenly erupts, just as I realize that I have made the fatal error of this place. *There is no empathy here, so don't try to find it.* In a blink, he's standing and shouting, his face purple. "Imagine what, boy?! I am a damn Sungate, this is where I was born, I'm not some malformed runt like you and those bitches in the Boroughs. My family name means something. Just because she keeps you as a pet, doesn't mean we want to hear your opinions!"

He spits on me then, and an anger rises in me that I cannot control. I am consumed by a hate so deep for this *thing* in front of me that I can only think to destroy it. He is not a man, he is the system that killed my friends and family, he is the mechanism that will keep killing them forever. He is the society that gives us their diseases, and then tells us to honor our dead. He is the structure that will keep us churning in that same meat grinder. I seethe as righteousness and rage burn through me. Without thinking, I launch myself towards him, and as if it's second nature my wings open and propel me forward. I grab his shirt collar, and with all the force I can muster I slam him into the balcony railing. I break him in half, and shatter it all.

Or, I try to. As we contact the railing, a force shield activates around the man, burning a beautiful cerulean blue. All the energy I put in, all that force, is reciprocated in an instant, and I'm launched backwards through the air, cartwheeling end over end.

Dorothy's after me the instant I take off, she knows already the end of this. She catches me in the air and we spin together. She slows us both with her wings. Once we've finally stopped tumbling, she grabs my arm, and we rocket downwards.

"We have to get you out of here, an assault like that will call the Centurions! You're safe outside of the district walls." She looks back over her shoulder, and my gaze follows hers. Inquisitors fly after us, their long, metallic fingers stretched out like knives in front of them. "Fuck, how'd they get here so soon?! We have to fly separately, the wings slow us down when we co-fly. I saw you back there, you know what to do, stay on my heels!"

She lets go of my arm, and I'm sure I'm fucked. What happened earlier was a fluke, driven solely by rage. But when she speeds off into a mass of people, I find that I somehow do know what to do, and I stay right behind her. We're flying straight towards heavy traffic, and the haptic feedback from my wings is going crazy.

"Close your eyes!" Dorothy screams.

I take a deep breath, close my eyes, and tune into it. With my eyes closed, it's like I can feel the shapes around me. I can see the trajectories of all the moving bodies. And with the slightest of motions, I naturally curve my body around to move through them.

I open my eyes on the other side and look back to see the Inquisitors slow down heavily to safely go around the column of traffic.

"They can't process as fast as we can."

We're back in the lower sea of swaying towers now. Outstretched verandas jut from them like claws of some slow moving beast, and we dodge and weave through it all at a speed that would kill us instantly if we hit. Suddenly, it comes into view. Dorothy holds up her hand and points to the gate we entered through. The exit back down to Cloud Spire.

As we're nearing the gate at a speed that seems unsafe to everyone around, the crowd starts to scream. I think it's about us, until I make out the words.

"CENTURIONS!!"

Right before we impact the ground, we both slow down enough to naturally move into a run. The guards have started to close the gate, but there's too many people running through, and we're able to break through with them. On the side of safety now, I spin around to see what's chasing us. I only briefly make out massive, hulking forms before the gate slams shut, leaving Dotty and I leaning on each other and breathing hard.

CHAPTER 11

As soon as I catch my breath, I start trying to apologize to Dotty. I feel like a fool, what seemed so righteous earlier just looks like the actions of a child now. But before I can get a word in, she starts laughing hysterically in between sucking in air.

"Holy shit, you tackled Edmond Sungate! The look on his face!"

"I know, Dotty, I'm so sorry—"

"Sorry? I would pay to see that happen again! He's a capital A *Asshole.* Wow, watching his face go from purple rage to the surprise of being manhandled! I needed that." She's wiping tears from her eyes. "Look, seriously we're lucky you got out. Inside the walls, actions like that are considered a threat against the system, and are dealt with *in totality.*"

Good to know. I realize I'm staring at her dumbfounded. "So if the Inquisitors had caught us?"

"They would have killed you, no questions asked. Even if you hadn't attacked Edmond, the Inquisitors were likely already closing in on you from the conversation you were having. You would have spent time in a cell regardless."

I'm shocked. "But, why? Is civil discourse not allowed inside the walls?"

She smiles again, but it's a very sad smile. "Because those in power write what they consider justice, why would they not do it in a way that keeps them in power? Civil discourse is encouraged, but only between those born in Sun Gate. For a lower to come with a competing viewpoint, well it reeks of revolution. They won't come for you outside the walls though, that's how you create martyrs for the people to follow." She grabs my arm and looks in my eyes then. "I'm sorry, I knew this could happen and I should have warned you. But I wanted you to fully understand what we're dealing with when we try to change the system. The monstrousness of it, the hugeness of it. I don't know how we tear it down. It all has to change."

In the time we've been talking, we've walked back to our tram. Joe has been waiting for us outside the gates. When he sees us approach, sweat stained, hair askew, and clothes ruffled he runs out to meet us.

"Sir Allen, my lady, is everything okay?"

"No problems, Joe, we just went for an unexpected jog."

Dorothy laughs at this and squeezes my arm. "I'm staying here, Allen. I need to untangle that mess back there so you're not still in danger."

I nod, and reach to my back to give her the wings back, but she puts a hand up to stop me.

"You can keep those, but they won't work outside the gate. They take power from the core of the city to work, just like everything in those walls. Consider it a reminder of our trip." I nod and bow, kissing her hand formally. She laughs and shakes her head, and pushing my arms aside hugs me hard. "Stay safe. I'll come over again soon," she whispers into my ear, and kisses my cheek. Then she whirls around, and heads back to the gate.

"Let's go home, Joe. I need a shower and a change of clothes."

For a time after, life takes on a wonderfully simple feel again. I pass my time in the gym, and reading on the library patio. Having seen inside Sun Gate now, I keep trying to think how I might infiltrate the medical facility, but it's like a wall that I keep hitting my head against. There were no visible doors, no discrete entry points. And with the level of technology outside the facility, what can I expect to find inside? If I had known all this before I started down this path it would have robbed me of purpose. Even now, with all the money and power available to me, I have no clue how to overcome it.

I'm deep in thought when my mother comes to join me on the veranda. She's wearing a lovely green summer dress and a large woven parasol hat. I can see tiny traces of dirt under her fingernails, and know that she's been working in the garden today.

"Darling, I haven't seen Dorothy around for some time. Is everything okay?"

I smile and close my book. "All fine, mother. She needs to do some things back home, you know how it is."

"Good, good. Well if she hasn't already asked you to attend the masked ball tonight with her, would you agree to accompany your mother? It's in the Skyball, and tons of politicals from Sun Gate will be there!"

For a second, I blanch at the thought of being near those hyenas again, or at running into Edmond. But a mask should provide a measure of anonymity, and being around them could provide me with more information. I wonder briefly why Dorothy *hasn't* invited me with her. *Is she concerned over my safety? And what is a Skyball?*

"I'd love to accompany you, mother, only I don't think I have a mask." *I'm so used to wearing this one, I think people will recognize me.*

"Oh lovely! And don't worry, I'll set one in your room. You can return to your reading, I'll see you this evening."

When I go back to my room later on, I find a beautiful, obsidian wolf's head mask lying on my bed. The edges of it are outlined in gold leaf, and the contrast makes the grimace look dangerous and mean.

I hold it up to my face and stare into the mirror. Robotic arms come out of my closet and hold up potential outfits while I stare out impassively from the wolf's visage. A great weariness hangs on me. *More parties, more balls, more galas...how will I ever change this place? People in the Boroughs are starving every single day while I sit idly on a veranda, drink wine, and eat my fill.* I want to smash the mask into the mirror then, to smash everything around me, but I check myself.

The arms bring out a dress uniform that fits the mask perfectly. It's black with golden epaulets and a double row of glistening, ornate buttons. The shoulders are comically sharp, and I straighten my back to meet their resolve. I pick it, and as the other outfits are being shuffled back away, the silver disc that Brian gave me falls from one of their pockets. I pick it up off the ground, and tuck it inside my evening attire. *May it remind me of the home that I've forsaken, and the people that I won't.*

I meet my mother and Joe on the landing pad. They are both dressed impeccably. My mother has on a lovely snow owl mask. Her dress is white and ruffled with shades of brown in a way that resembles plumage. Joe is unmasked, but sharp in a fresh tuxedo. He's polished the tram into a glistening, brilliant thing. We load in, and join a line of others heading up and towards Sun Gate.

I can see the Skyball through the wide view window at the front. I've noticed it before, but thought it was just a false moon. As we get closer, I see that it's an entirely transparent ball that hangs from the top of the city. It shimmers grandly with silver and glass. There's an entry port and landing for trams on the bottom, where a series of lifts take guests up to the main level at the center of the sphere.

Joe expertly pilots our carriage through the queue, and lands smoothly in the thick of a forest of other trams. We're close enough to Sun Gate here that I feel the wings on my neck start to stir, but not close enough to fully wake them. Joe swings open our passenger door, and helps my mother out. As I get out, Joe bows to us.

There's a menagerie around us, and I get lost just looking around at it. There are different animal masks everywhere, I can't recognize any of the people behind them. As I look closer, I see that some of the masks give away a bit more of the facial features, while some cover the entire head and create the impression of a walking abomination.

We join the funnel of people up the lifts to the main ballroom. Out of the floor, banisters spring to surround the lift. It rises seamlessly, carrying the huge crowds upwards. It's easily a hundred feet to the next level, and as we go up I watch Joe slowly shrink to a dot in the crowd beneath us.

"Isn't it beautiful up here?" my mother asks with a grand sigh as we rise into the main ballroom.

I forget to respond, I'm too overwhelmed. Everything around us is built from the same transparent glass, and reflected light glints everywhere. As the lifts reach the main level, the floor turns opaque, sealing us off in this shimmering half dome. Glass chandeliers hang from the ceiling, sending colors everywhere as they slowly rotate. A second level rings half of the ballroom, a small veranda that looks out over everything.

"Oh, how lovely! I'm going to mingle, have fun darling." My mother immediately disappears towards the center of the ballroom. I spy a passing waiter, and grab a glass of wine from his tray. I slowly walk the exterior of the room, trying to see if I can recognize anyone.

As I'm walking the room, a man standing at a small cocktail table apart from the party waves me down. He's wearing a tuxedo and top hat, but is unmasked and leaning on a cane. As I get closer, I see his dark eyes sparkle out from his craggy face with a deep intelligence and cunning. The depth to his eyes shocks me. Curious, I approach.

"Hail! Greetings, good sir. What a wonderful replica of 19th century naval uniforms that is," he says, his voice a raspy croaking thing.

I tilt my head at him, entirely unsure of what the words mean.

"Ahhh don't mind me, I read too much history and assume others do as well."

"Not many have access to history books," I reply. It's true, even in my father's library there's scant historical information.

"And fewer have the interest to read them! For most, there's only the immediacy of the now. But I'd wager that we'd all learn something from knowing what we are, and where we came from. It brings such lovely clarity to things, I find."

"So you know what came before, then?" I ask, incredibly interested.

"Aye son, but it's privileged information. I wish I could tell you more now, but I bet that you'll learn it in time."

I nod, and as the conversation lapses we both turn and watch the room. *What a strange man, and what a strange response. Learn it in time?* People have started to dance with random partners, and there are small groups in conversation all over the floor. A massively rotund man in a walrus mask stands nearby, and I immediately recognize his form. *At least it's easy to tell where Edmond is.*

"Ahhh, it is refreshing to watch. The dancing, the liveliness, the fun. I've lived too long, I think. The pain has all mixed with the pleasure until I can't tell them apart anymore." His words draw me back, but he's as much talking to himself as me. He's lost in some internal reverie, there's a distant look on his face. "I wonder some days what the point is. Every day, the same things. I just want to experience something definitively new, but there's nothing new left for me. The man at the center of the universe sees it all, but is touched by nothing." He lets out an exasperated sigh.

"How old are you, sir, if you don't mind me asking?"

"Nearly two centuries, son. Or maybe it's longer than that, I stopped keeping track so long ago. Maybe we weren't intended to live this long." Behind my mask, my mouth hangs open in shock.

Suddenly an arm interlaces with mine, and I turn around to be greeted by a woman in a white evening gown, a snow fox mask on her face. She's wearing a loose fitting white dress that is tied behind her neck. It rolls over her curves beautifully, accentuating and defining them, and drawing my eyes to their highlights. Her skin stands out a beautiful brown against the color. I'd recognize her anywhere.

"Excuse me sir, do you mind if I borrow him?" Dorothy says.

The old man bows slightly, and turns away. Dorothy guides me away, towards the staircase that leads to the second level.

"Was it so easy to spot me then?"

She laughs, and leaning in closer whispers into my ear. "I'd like to think that I can recognize certain qualities of yours behind any mask." She pinches my rear, and I chuckle and shake my head.

She guides me up the stairs. Before we step on each one, they turn briefly opaque so we can see them fully.

"I saw Edmond down there."

She nods. "I think it's best if you two don't spend much time together." She suddenly turns serious. "To be honest, I didn't think you'd be here at all."

"And miss an opportunity to mix with my favorite blood-thirsty hyenas? I couldn't do that!"

We're at the top of the veranda now, and find it empty. Everyone is down below, being loud and getting drunker by the minute.

Despite the noise, Dotty keeps her voice down. I have to lean in to hear her. "Listen, it's not safe here for you, Allen. If you take the lift down, no one will notice you." There's genuine concern in her voice, and fear too.

"Oh, I'm sure they won't realize it's me, and anyways we're outside of Sun Gate here. You said it yourself, they wouldn't try anything out here. So what's the worst that could happen? A hangover?"

As if the universe chooses this one time to respond to my question, my world shatters around me just after I ask it. The sound of crashing and splintering glass rips through the ballroom, and we immediately crouch and I throw up an arm to shield us from any shrapnel. When I lower it, I see three trams have been driven through the beautiful, flawless roof of the Skyball. There are battering rams on the front of them, reinforced metal meant to drive like a wedge into the building.

The glass has fallen right where I stood with the old man. I look for his body in the wreckage, expecting to see his bloody corpse, but I can't see him. *I wonder if this is the new experience he was after.*

The trams spin down and land, as the crowd screams and runs clear. Out of them pours twelve of the most demonic figures I've ever seen. They wear matching black cloaks that billow loosely around them, the hood of the cloaks meld seamlessly into a top hat and a bizarre white mask. It has a beak on it that extends out from their faces, and mirrored goggles block their eyes. A tube extends from the end of their beaks back into their cloaks.

For a moment, I consider that this is a poorly executed joke. For a moment, I convince myself that everything is okay. Dotty and I have stood back up, and are backing away from the veranda edge slowly.

"HELLO THERE, YOU FUCKING COWARDS!!"

The voice comes from one of them, but it's amplified over speakers in the trams. It echoes all around us, and the volume crushes my eardrums. Realization hits me, it's the Plague Doctors. I look around for an exit, but the closest is a lift at the bottom of the stairs.

"WE HEARD THERE WAS A PARTY WITH ALL OUR FAVORITE MURDERERS AND FUCKWITS. IT SOUNDED LIKE A GAS TO US!"

This is the cue, and they all lift their arms and toss smoking spheres into the crowd.

"GAS MASKS!" Dotty screams at me and flips something on her own mask. I stare dumbly at her—mine certainly doesn't have that feature. She grabs my shoulders and shakes me out of my stupor, and the disc Brian gave me slaps against my chest. I reach in and push the button, but the green gas is already spreading across the veranda. The shield goes up over my face just as that gas hits us.

Too fucking slow. It's burning my eyes and caught in my throat, and I'm on the ground coughing. I hear chaos underneath us as people run for the lifts.

"THAT'S A REAL CURIOUS THING OUR LAB RATS BUILT, A FAST-ACTING PLAGUE. DEPENDING ON HOW MUCH OF IT YOU JUST INHALED, YOU'LL ALL BE DEAD IN THE NEXT FIVE TO TEN MINUTES. GOOD LUCK, IT WAS TERRIBLE TO KNOW YOU, I HOPE IT HURTS AT THE END!"

The room echoes with their laughter, and it pulses across my head like a hammer. Dotty hauls me to my feet and screams in my ear. "We have to go now!"

Suddenly, silence descends over the room, like everyone has stopped to stare at something. I look up in time to see behemoth, four-armed monsters leaping through the hole in the ceiling. They're covered in glistening black armor, and grapple lines extend from their hands to guide the descent. They come down like a silent death, quiet and inescapable. The first one drops his line thirty feet in the air, and smashes into the floor right behind one of the Plague Doctors. It stands easily double his height, its massive body hulking over the cloaked figure. In an instant, the beast has lifted him off the ground, ripped one of his arms off, and crumpled his body like it was an empty sack.

"CENTURIONS, GAS 'EM BOYS!"

CHAPTER 12

Broken from our stupor, we run for the lifts. We just gain the bottom landing as the crowd surges on. I see my mother force her way on, and we start the slow descent. The ballroom is a war zone. Bodies are scattered everywhere I look, some people are still rushing to get to a lift, and in the center of it all the Plague Doctors spar with four massive Centurions.

Looking at them in full view now, I feel like a fever has already taken hold of my brain. They're freakish, probably double my height, and everything seems to have scaled proportionally. A single hand could easily wrap around my head, which is confirmed when I watch one of them do this to a Doctor. Their head is crushed like a blueberry. The second set of arms seems to make no anatomical sense. They protrude right underneath the correctly placed pair, the same size and available movement patterns. I keep having to blink as I watch the four arms move, as if it's a trick I'm seeing that shouldn't be there.

How do these things exist? Where are they from? Are we even the same fucking species? It's all wrong.

Besides their heads, they're completely covered in a glistening black armor that I've never seen. But what heads they are. More than anything else, that's what gives me pause. They're huge of course, in fitting with the rest of their bodies. What bothers me is the faces. They are all the exact same, perfect replicas of each other. Their dark eyes are deeply set, and stare out impassively. Besides the occasional mark of pain, there is no emotion on their face.

It's like staring into the face of an Inquisitor. Completely blank and devoid of any real life. They look just like the images of cattle I've seen.

One of the Doctors pulls out a plasma sword and slashes at the great beast's leg. Smoke pours from the armor, and although it eventually makes it through, it's slowed enough that the Doctor has been grabbed and tossed across the room like a doll.

In total, eight of the Doctors are dead or severely wounded. Of the four Centurions that stormed the ballroom, one is puking blood and another lies motionless with a plasma sword in his eye. I can see that the remaining Centurions are slowing as they start to succumb to the gas, and it reminds me that we're next.

As the lift finally descends out of view of the main ballroom, one of the trams lifts off and crashes through the wall of the Skyball. It sends huge glass shards cascading down onto a full lift on the other side of the room.

The speed of the lift, which seemed to move with a gracious slowness on our ascent, is now a knife twisting in all of our guts.

The speed is killing us, all of us, and all we can do is wait. As their symptoms worsen, people push and shove on the lift, and within moments a few of them close to the railing have been pushed over the edge. I watch them careen over the side, and hear their short screams suddenly get cut off at the landing.

Blood covers the lift opposite ours, where the glass crashed down moments ago. People hang from the railings, motionless and dripping. I see a few of them are still moving there, but I can't imagine they will be for long.

All around me the plague has taken a deep hold. Some are already passed out on the floor of the lift, covered in the vomited blood of others as they're trampled to death. Dotty and I are an island in the middle of it all, stabilizing off of each other and doing everything we can to stay afloat. I spin around and see that I'm standing next to Edmond. He's shed his walrus mask and has blood streaming from his mouth and nose. I panic for a moment, realizing my mask was knocked off, but then realize I still have my disease shield up so he can't see my face.

Some of the others also have masks that filter gas. I can see the clever engineering of them up close now. It's clear not all of them got the timing right, as I watch them rip the masks off to throw up blood. Dotty seems unaffected, thankfully, but as I watch those around me I know my time is coming. The disease shield must have saved me from a full exposure, but it won't matter.

Fever chills wrack me, and I shiver uncontrollably. I haven't been sick in so long that it feels strangely foreign now. *Is this how it was in the past? Is this worse?* As the lift slowly descends, I calmly note the progress. First, the fever worsens and I start to disconnect from reality. Then I taste blood in my mouth, and see a black lesion growing on the back of my arm. When the lift finally touches down, I vomit blood for the first time. Dorothy wraps her arm around my neck, and carries me towards the tram.

What's she trying to do? Just leave me. There's no fixing this.

I try to speak, but nothing comes out except mumbles. Dorothy helps me stumble along, and we find my mother leaning against a tram nearby. Dorothy grabs her too, and when Joe spots us he rushes over to help.

"Holy shit, what happened?!"

"Gas. Plague. They die in minutes, Joe," Dorothy gets out between ragged breaths.

He pales, and even in my sick state I can see that something is also dying inside him now.

"Joe, you know what the contract states," My mother barely gets the words out, long pauses separating each of them as she speaks. She's leaning against our tram for support and looks about to collapse.

"Aye, miss, I do. I just, please miss, don't make little Josephine take his place! She's just a little girl, she still has a bright future!" He's pointing at me, and I can see the terror in his eyes.

My mother stands to her full stature, somehow holding herself up one last time. "Do not plead with me, Joe. You have been with us for too long and you know the price. Your life for mine, your girl's for his. You agreed to it. If you break your word, you'll be a pariah, and our family will make sure you both starve to death." Her piece spoken, she slumps back against the tram.

Joe is crying, distraught. Through the brain-melting fever, the pieces start to fall into place. *Joe's contract must state that in the event of terminal illness, he trades places with us, and his daughter—that beautiful little happy thing with pigtails—she's bound by the same thing. I'm sick of it, sick of these fucking monsters that would kill a girl for me. FOR ME. For no more reason than we have money.*

I think about that innocent thing trading her life for mine. I see her pigtails bouncing as she sits down at the Box, and it pushes everything evil that's inside me into her. She doesn't just die. She suffers. *What sort of fucking justice is this world after. My family didn't keep them close because they cared about them. They kept them close as an insurance policy.* I'm so disgusted by it that I want to just lie down and stop existing. This world is beyond fixing, and I'd rather die than continue trying to live in it.

"I will not let that little girl die so I can live!" I throw Dotty's arms off me and try to run. I will not keep using people like these monsters do. I don't care if I fail my mission, I don't care if this city keeps eating itself. *Eat your fucking hearts out monsters, I will have no part.* Brian was right, of course he was. It's not worth selling my humanity to this thing.

In my head, Allen's memories of Josephine start to swirl. I see her at a family party, laughing and jubilant. I see Joe teaching her to drive. I see Allen giving her a ride on his back as she screams in pure happiness. There's a sudden feeling of cohesion between us, like we've been brought into full alignment. *I will not hurt that child.*

I know I'm dead, and I figure if I can make it to the edge and jump that will make it final. It will be mercifully quick. It looms in the distance, and I give everything I have to get there. Only, I can't run, I can barely crawl.

Dotty hauls me off the ground, but keeps moving away.

"Where? Don't make me kill Josephine." I get out. My mother is screaming incoherently after us, but we keep moving away.

"I won't. My driver is here," she says, straining against my weight.

"Take me to Brian's then. I want to die with friends."

She's crying, so she just nods. And then her driver is there, and I'm being tossed into the back of a tram. And the world is swimming, swirling above me. There's no pain or fear anymore, but also no sudden moment of clarity. I'm hot and something like drunk and so, so tired. And I know I'm dying. I really want to close my eyes, but Dotty is slapping my face and screaming...something. I say nice things back to her, or I try to. I tell her it's okay, I'm not really Allen, I'm just a fraud that fell in love with her while trying to change everything. She doesn't have to cry over me. I just wanted everyone I love to be happy and safe.

For a while, I drift in the current. There's a swirl of vision, Dotty's face drifts through it, and lights bounce all around. It's hard to understand if I'm awake. It's hard to understand much at all, thinking feels thick and slow. Sometimes I think I'm talking, trying to tell her something important. There are some words I've wanted to say, but I keep getting confused along the way.

There's a sudden blast of cold air, and my eyes spring back open for a moment. I see Brian's face, I've never seen him so serious. I tell him he's the best man I know, I tell him I love him and I always will. And it's okay to let me go. I tell him I'm sorry for all the shit I've put him through. I'm a bad friend but I had to try and make it better here. Only he doesn't seem to hear it, and he rushes off and I close my eyes again.

Stainless steel and lights. I hear the familiar noises of the hospital. The beeping that monitors my heart sounds slowed and erratic. I was always meant to die here. I escaped it once, somehow, but now I'm back. I've never felt more tired in my life, so I close my eyes.

And that's it. The end. I let go and I drift on the currents.

There's a feeling that starts in my soul. Right there at my very core. There is this thing that starts pulling all the pain and misery out of me. Piece by piece. And everything it touches feels better. Everything it touches feels whole and right in a way it never has.

Is this it, the end? Is there peace after all of that?

The feeling keeps building and building, and soon there is a peacefulness in me that I could never find in life. The constant pain, the sickness, the hunger, the lying. None of it mattered, there was always going to be peace afterwards. I couldn't fix the world, but at least there's this. I feel transcendent and glorious.

The thought soothes me, and I float away on it.

CHAPTER 13

Slowly, I return to my body. My eyes open, and I'm confused. *I died, but I'm still in this damn hospital.* I look down at my body, my hospital gown is caked in vomited blood. There's a tube protruding from my chest, and it looks so familiar. It scratches something in my brain, but everything is so fogged over that the thought keeps getting lost.

I follow the tube up with my eyes, and see it end in a giant metal box. The box is perfect, the reflective silver corners of it are crisp and faultless. *What a big box this is. Big. Metal. Box. The Box. Oh fuck the Box. Of fuck, no, no, no.* Adrenaline shoots through me and I bolt upright. I swing my feet over the edge of the bed I'm on, and on the other side of the Box there are legs sticking out of a chair. The Box blocks the person from view. There's another tube on that side—I know the misery that comes out of the end of that tube too well.

I have to know. I don't want to know. I hear a choked cry, and realize it's from me. I try to get off the bed and just fall to the floor. As I'm trying to push myself back up, warm arms wrap around my waist and help me up.

It's Dotty, and I'm so relieved to see her but so devastated for what it means. For who it means is on the other end of that tube. I'm trying to move over there, and I'm already crying, but she holds me back.

"Lay down, you need more rest."

"No, I need to know," I croak through a throat that seems to barely work, it feels full of cotton.

She hangs her head and walks me to the other side of the machine, and my world breaks. Brian, my greatest friend, the father I always needed, is dead and pale in the chair with a tube strapped to his chest.

My legs fold underneath me and I fall from her arms. I can't stop shaking.

"You fucking idiot! You weren't supposed to die! I was supposed to die! You hate the Box, you would never use it!" I scream at him through tears. His silence is deafening. Dotty is sitting behind me. She's holding me and rocking me. She's saying things to me but I can't listen.

Two thoughts chase themselves in my brain, bouncing end over end.

Brian's dead. It's your fault. Brian's dead. It's your fault. Brian's dead. It's your fault.

"He chose this. He knew we couldn't save you and he chose this immediately. Without question." She's trying to console me but I shake my head.

In my memory, Brian calls me an idiot the first time I came to his hospital. He does the same thing, again and again, as we get progressively older together. He offers wisdom, and care. He pulls his chair next to my bed, and in his face I find the one place of stability that I have. I met him when I lost my father, and he'd filled that void since then.

"No, no no no, fuck. THIS. FUCK THIS." I punch the ground, and the pain brings me back to myself. "He was the best man I knew, he's saved so many. And what am I? Just some kid that's done nothing. Contributed nothing. A fucking waste. I'm not worth him. Dammit, why didn't he just let me die?!"

"Because he loved you too," she says it, and it cuts through me. Makes me stop. I know it's the truth, only I never put words to it. *I was the son he didn't have.* I sit back and for a long time I just cry, and she holds me. And she's crying too, though she barely knew him.

At some point, Dorothy leaves and returns with the clothes that I was wearing. They're in a folded pile, with my wolf mask on top. She sets it on the floor next to me, and I pick up the mask and stare into its face. I stare through those hollow eyes.

Asking a wolf to be decent while it's currently eating a lamb sounds like an approach that disregards what the lamb wants entirely. The words echo through my memory.

I won't be a lamb anymore. If they're wolves, I'd rather be a hunter.

I toss the mask to the side and look at the uniform. Dotty has done what she can to clean it, but blood still stains it. I notice it's missing a few buttons too, but it adds to the austerity of it. Like me, it's been through battle.

I pull the clothes on and look at myself in the reflection of the Box. I'm a frightening visage. Unsmiling and blood stained, warped by the reflection. I stare into the cold metal and see these past months.

I've tried the slow approach. I've tried to gather information and friends. It's overwhelming, there's no way I can succeed from this direction. There's no way I can succeed by continuing to bargain my humanity. This whole place is sick, and I need to be the surgeon that's willing to cut in and excise it. The only way forward is through, I just have to act.

"Dotty, I haven't been entirely honest with you." Her head whips up to stare at me, eyes narrowing. "Since I came back, I've been trying to find a way to tear this whole system down. It's the chains the society uses to oppress, the shackles that keep the poor bound to us. We make parasites out of them, so they can suck out our poison."

I pause, and see all the people that have died in its wake. I see my family ripped apart when my father died. I see Joe resigning himself to die to save a woman that will never deserve that. I see his daughter Josephine, with all the happiness of youth, under contract for her life to end at any point. I see Brian. *Fucking Brian*, the best of them. Dead now, to save me.

"I'm done not acting. I'm done moving slowly." I turn and stare into her eyes, they're focused on me intently. She's not moving, barely blinking, absorbing everything I'm saying. "I'm going to find a way into that damn building, and tear the guts out of this thing for good. This has to end. I don't care if I smash myself apart on the rocks. I will not have Brian die to save me, and then do nothing to change this world."

She looks away for a time with tears in her eyes. And when she looks back, the smiling, laughing, beautiful woman is gone. She looks ferocious and frightening, with a wicked grin and shining eyes.

"Good, I've been wondering what your game was. Now since we're being fully honest, I've been working on the same thing since our trip to Sun Gate."

She's with me. She's a real ally now. The pain for continuing to lie to her tears deeper in that instant than it ever has. She may be the best friend I have left in this world, and she doesn't even really know who I am. I want so badly to tell her the truth then—she's my greatest betrayal and the shame of it is overwhelming.

This lie to her cheapens my resolve. Brian would tell me to come clean and I know it. I want to stop using her, but I can't see this all crash down around me. Not now. Not after everyone that's died. I can only offer her a silent atonement. *No matter what happens, I won't let you die too. Even if I have to sacrifice myself.*

"Look, I'm sick of trying to change things diplomatically, I don't want to wait years for the results of some damn 'decency campaign' when people are being used up every single day. I feel so idle, so fucking useless. Without politicals on our side, there's nothing left to do but act directly. So I figured out a way to use my dad's biolock, and I have a general idea where we need to go. But Allen, do you know what infiltration looks like?"

I shake my head, surprised that she's already started to plan.

"I've been inside just once, with my father. We went through several layers of security checkpoints to even get there, and then the place was crawling with Inquisitors and Centurions. Did you think four of them was a fearsome sight last night? Their entire barracks is somewhere in that tower. We'd need an army to get in there, and we'd probably lose most of them."

I think for a few moments, considering our options. I have a monstrous thought, and as much as I want nothing to do with them, I can't see another way.

"I know an army that might be interested."

In the Boroughs, we have no special way to honor our dead. People die, and are incinerated. There's no space for bodies that aren't living, and certainly none for graves or mausoleums. I know such things were done in the past, before the city, but it's hard for me to imagine why. We feed them to the flames, and tell each other stories of their lives.

The hospital incinerator is a lonesome affair. It's packed into a tiny space at the end of the hall on the lower level. The room is smaller than my closet in Cloud Spire. I have no idea if Brian honored the dead he brought here, but I'm certain he was the only one present when they were fed into the flames. There's barely room for Dotty and I, so we have to stand shoulder to shoulder staring into the mouth of the great beast. Brian is laid out in front of us.

I did my best to make him look peaceful. Dying from plague is not an easy end, and it showed. There were blood stains and lesions all over his body. I find a fresh lab coat, the only thing I think I ever saw him wear, and we dress him in it. I have to stop several times to cry, but I owe this to my friend and I won't back away from it.

So we recount the stories of his life, and most of them I can't say out loud, so I only say them in my head.

"You saved me when I was brought here. I should have died."

You saved countless generations of us from dying from a system of sickness. You were a hero.

"You opened the doors of your hospital and showed me the devastation of life down here," Dotty adds.

"You gave me a shield that likely saved my life."

You gave me your loyalty and friendship, always. You nurtured me, helped me grow, and when I left my home you supported me from afar. You were my truest friend.

"You hated the system, but never blamed people for working in it."

"You were my friend." I place my hand on his feet, and start to feed him into the flames.

You were the father I never had at home. I'll love you friend, and remember you always.

Dotty joins in, and we push him into the incinerator. As the mouth of the great beast opens and accepts him, we watch the flames lick his body. They cover every part of him, and it's beautiful. The mouth of the incinerator closes, but I can still see the flames with my eyes closed. A part of me wishes that I could always see them there, behind my eyelids. A memory preserved, but one only I can see.

Afterwards, Dotty and I discussed our plans for some time. She has a way that we can use her father's biolock, but it's at her family home. I've asked her to discreetly grab a few items from my house in Cloud Spire as well—I have no plans to go back there. I don't want to look in my mother's eyes again. I'd only think of Joe and that thought makes me sick.

Meanwhile, I have an arms dealer to locate. I never got their information from Brian, but if they're as loud as he suggested, it shouldn't be too difficult. I know this place. These *lower levels* were once my home. It's time to kick the dust in my old haunts, and try to find this damn rat.

We pick out a meeting spot, and a message that I'll send her when I'm ready. And then we set it all in motion. She kisses me like it's for the last time, and leaves the hospital to find a public tram.

Before I leave, I look at myself in the mirror of an empty room. I see the man I was in the Boroughs, I see the man who lived in the clouds, and I see this new man, resurrected and full of rage. I've died twice, but I won't give up. We're both here, Allen and Nick, but now we're together. The weight of the disease shield is in my pocket, and like a token from the dead, it feels full of meaning.

May it remind me of the home that I've forsaken, and the people that I won't. May it remind me that my aims are not worth bargaining my humanity for. May I carry your weight with me always, my good friend.

Before I go find this dealer, there's someone else I need to visit first.

It's not hard to find her home. I ask around in Meadow Hearth—there aren't many places with a Cloud Spire tram, and only one whose ownership recently switched to an orphan. People down here loved Joe. When I ask about him, their eyes shift down in sadness.

"Gone too soon, he was a good man. Gave me a ride to the hospital when I broke my hip," a woman in a teacher's uniform says, her arms full of thick books. She shakes her head as she hobbles away.

"Poor girl, we all been there but I ain't sayin' that makes it okay," a man with a gap tooth frown tells me when I ask for directions on their block. "I run a food stall down the way, used to see 'em both there for dinner. Always happy, always smiling. Poor girl."

Their home isn't much better than the hovels in the Boroughs. Two stories tall, a living space on top of an open garage, but squeezed into a tiny footprint that's barely wider than the tram parked below. The walls are metal, but tarnished and stained like everything else here.

My heart's pounding when I knock on the door. I have no clue what I'll say to her, no clue what she even knows already. There's a slow shuffle from behind it, and then the door creaks open on corroded hinges.

For an instant, I see the smiling girl with blonde pigtails that bounce behind her when the door opens, but it's just a memory. She's been replaced by a young girl with slumped shoulders that's being crushed under the weight of our world. Josephine's eyes are bloodshot from crying, her blonde hair is thrown back in a messy ponytail. When she raises her eyes up to meet mine, they grow wide with a terrible recognition. Then she bolts through the door and hugs me around my waist, and I feel her sobbing.

I realize self-consciously that I'm still wearing my blood-stained clothes from the Sky Ball. I wish I had thought to change them, and at least shield this girl from some of the horror of that night.

"Da said you died, Sir Allen!" She gets out between sobs.

"A good friend sacrificed himself for me," I say, gently pushing her away from me so I can kneel and talk to her eye to eye. I reach up and brush the tears from her face.

"My da..."

"I know. I'm so sorry, munchkin. He deserved to live," I say, and she sobs again. "I came to apologize for my family, and—"

"Da called me before, he, you know. Said to remember you as a great man, said because of you I get to live," she says through the tears.

"My life wasn't worth yours, Josephine. It wasn't worth the man who gave me his, either. And my mom's certainly wasn't worth your dad's. This whole system is garbage. I wanted you to know I'm going to try and break it. But before I go, I need to give you something." I reach down to my screen and key in numbers. Once it's ready I show it to her, and her eyes grow wide. "This is enough for you to live well for years, if you're careful with it. Please, stop working for my family. Break your contract, don't let them take you too." I post-date the transaction so it won't go through immediately. My *parents* will likely cut off my account when it does and I need some time before they do. Then I hold my screen out to her.

"It's the only thing I know how to do. It's what my da taught me," she says, and I know the weight of what she means.

"You're not betraying him, he just wanted you to have a good life."

She nods at this with fresh tears in her eyes, and holds her screen up to meet mine. There's a soft chime as the transaction confirms. A small weight lifts from me with it. I can't bring Joe back, but at least I can save his daughter the same fate.

"I might not see you for a while, Josephine. Please, take care—"

She runs forward and hugs me again, nearly knocking me over. I hug her back fiercely. Then I stand and give her a nod. Both of our eyes are filled with tears.

"Goodbye for now, Sir Allen," she says, and walks back into her house, softly closing the door behind her.

Be safe, little one.

Now, it's time to work.

I visit the Metal Oyster first. Brian never sent me any information on this arms dealer he'd known, but I know he likes to talk. So I go where the talkers go to spin their stories—the Oyster feels as good a place as any. When I walk in, the host recognizes my face, and he starts to offer me a welcoming smile. But then he sees my clothes, and he freezes somewhere in between a greeting and wanting to run.

"A seat at the bar," I growl when he says nothing for several moments.

He snaps his mouth shut, returning to reality, and walks me over to the bar. He's unsure whether to sit me next to the drunks, and clearly too uncomfortable to ask. I walk past him and choose a seat far enough away that it's clear I don't want to talk, but I can still hear the conversation at the other end. The barman comes over immediately.

"Yes sir, hullo sir, what will it be tonight sir?"

"Don't call me sir. What are they drinking?" I thumb toward the other group.

"Oh, well they're drinking block wine. It's made from those nutrient blocks all the lowers eat, pretty flavorless stuff, probably someone of your caliber wouldn't—"

"That's fine, I'll take one."

The barman's mouth is open for a moment, and then he closes it and nods. He turns, and pours a tall mug full of a brown liquid from a spigot behind the bar. He places it in front of me, and not knowing what else to say, walks away.

There was a time I used to see my Dad drinking block wine with his friends, back before he got really sick. He'd brew it in the house in a small tarp covered barrel and the whole place stank of fermentation back then. When it was ready, he'd sit on the porch sharing it out to other Sickos and they'd all drink until the barrel was dry. Back then, it was always exciting when my Dad got drunk. It felt like we were living a more lavish life. Of course, I'd sneak some of it too when he wasn't looking. The taste was horrible but I loved feeling like one of his friends. I'd tried the stuff a few times since then, but the taste had too much memory for me.

This block wine is better than what my Dad made, but there's only so good the stuff can be. There's a mild sweetness to it at first that masks a more bitter taste underneath, but then the burn of the alcohol hits my throat and that's all I can taste. I sip it slowly while I listen to the conversation.

"Did you boys hear what Dan went and did?"

"Nope, haven't seen him in an age. He broke again?"

"He took a big one. Cancer. Made it work so his family will be good for a long time."

"That's gonna be the end of the road for all of us. Good man to set his family up. How bad is it?"

"Stage 4, he's not even going to the hospital. Just waiting it out at home."

The others nod, and I realize my eyes have been sucked over to them. I wonder if that was Dan we saw signing his life away here the other night. I don't think my mark is here, so I type something into my screen and then signal to the barman.

When he walks over I show him the screen on my arm, it's enough money to cover his expenses for a month. His eyes grow wide looking at it.

"I'm looking for someone that sells *defensively*, likes to run his mouth. Maybe you've heard of him, maybe he's been here. Know anything?" I say it quietly, so the others can't hear.

The barman nods, and after grabbing a bottle of whiskey behind the bar, pours out a thimble for me. He's giving cover to answering my question, I realize, and play along. When he pushes the tiny glass over he says "Try the Dead Parrot, I heard of your boy from a friend of mine over there."

I nod and take the whiskey down, and then we grasp our screens together in a forearm shake. It's one of many ways to transfer funds, but the preferred way in the lower levels. He's shocked to see I know it, so I wink at him, and leave. Spending money will certainly let my parents in Cloud Spire know that I'm still alive, but they might not notice this low of a payment for some time.

The Dead Parrot is one of several very rowdy bars inside of the Red Light district. It's a squat, windowless building with a neon sign that shows a sideways parrot with x's over the eyes. Allen knows this place, I feel it stirring in my memory. Nothing is off limits here. You can buy and take Luna freely, find women and men for the night, or just drink until you find oblivion. It's full of people looking to do the same.

The walk into the Red Light district is littered with barely dressed people, selling their wares. People in the lower levels don't shame them for it, they're just trying to put food on the table like the rest of us. No one in the lower levels has money for it, anyways. The people here are commonly abused, or worse, by the rich that come down to this neighborhood for a night of debauchery. Some mornings, a body will be found in the street, used up and left there. Inquisitors don't come down for stuff like that. It's an incredibly sad place to be.

I ignore some harassment from them as I walk to the Parrot, but mostly I'm also ignored. The blood stains on my uniform do a good job of discouraging people's interest in spending a night with me. The front of the Parrot is empty. No one wants to mix with the crowd leaving this place, but the light from the doorway tells me it's open. I take a deep breath, and enter.

There's thick, cloying tobacco smoke spread across everything inside. A few heads look up and take me in, but seem unconcerned. I'm certainly not the first person to come in with blood stains on their clothes. I take a seat at the bar. The barman sees me, and without asking, pours a thimble of whiskey and brings it over.

"I heard yous was coming."

"Word travels fast."

"Aye, you a paying customer?" He looks down at my screen, and I nod. I'm sure the barman from the Metal Oyster told him how many credits I spilled.

"Pay attention to them cats in the corner." He points them out with a slight shift to his eyes. I follow his gaze, and see a table of two tucked in the corner. Both men are slight, but one is bent so far to be nearly flopped on the table. The other sits tall and proud. I cue up some money on my screen, and transfer it to the barman. Then I grab my whiskey and take an empty table where I can just barely hear their conversation.

"—caused quite a mess."

"Stiffen your back, man, you knew what we were about." Shivers run down my spine at his voice, and it's everything I have to not leap up and shove my hidden knife into the man. I heard that voice the night before, at maximum volume, as the person behind it tossed poison gas into a crowd of people. Brian would be alive if not for that person.

"I don't know if I do, actually. This is a massive escalation. Did you have help on the inside?"

"Piss off, this is what we've always been about. Maximum damage, kill the oppressors, burn it all down."

He sounds like me before I lived in the clouds, entirely without empathy for those up there. Willing to hurt whoever to change it. It's almost funny to hear it from someone else. I spent time in their world, and it changed me. I found some remnants of humanity there. They're just trying to find ways to keep living, and they're given the cruelest tools to do it. But it's destroying their souls, just like it's destroying the bodies of everyone in the Boroughs. They sold off their humanity, but if I take away the tools, maybe they can find it again.

"Well now, what am I supposed to do? *Inquisitors* will come looking soon enough." Even from here, I can hear the fear in his voice.

"Haha, if you think they're bad, wait until you see a Centurion. You should have seen us—"

"Don't brag to me, boy. I have to go into hiding thanks to you."

"Oh come on, you know you're welcome in the ratway. Ain't no Inquisitor that will find us down there."

"You know I can't find new business down there, right?"

"Don't sound like it matters much, if it's only the business of dying that you'll find up here."

There's an exasperated sigh, and I hear one of them get up. "Fine. I'll contact you. I need to buy some security first." The stooped man walks past me and exits the Parrot. I wait as long as I can, so that the other doesn't know I'm after his friend, and then I casually get up and follow. By the time I'm out in the street, he's nowhere to be seen.

Damn. Where did that bastard run off to? Did he notice me on his way out?

I rush down the street in one direction, and then the other, staring into alleys and looking for his stooped frame. People are starting to stare at me, but I don't care. I keep seeing him in every one I pass, but when I stop them, it's not him. *Fuck, I can't give myself away like this, I need to slow down.*

I stop running and just breathe. The adrenaline of the moment leaves me, and I realize just how tired I am. I've lost him for now. I need a place to sleep and think. *It's time to go home, finally.*

It's strange, sitting across the table from my ma. I'm an alien in a place that used to be familiar, but feels different now. It's that way everywhere now, it seems. The walls seem closer, the table feels smaller, and everything looks dirtier than it did in my memory. There's a steaming cup of nutrient tea in front of me. I sip it slowly, and the taste of it with the smell of this place brings such a deep feeling of comfort that I close my eyes and breathe in deeply.

"I can't believe ya look like this now, son. What a change, what a change," ma says, and my eyes snap back open.

When she answered the door, her voice caught in her throat at the sight of me. Like she was trying to say hello, but only a small squeak came out. She threw open her arms and hugged me fiercely. I had to coax her to let me in off the street, I still didn't want to be seen.

"I know it, the process was horrible. It nearly took me a month of bedrest to recover, I've never felt that much pain before."

My ma shakes her head at this, so I don't go any further.

"But why'd you do it? Were you tired of living here, with me?"

I stare around the room before I respond. I see the chair where my da used to sit, before we lost him. Memories race across my vision. I see the three of us laughing at this table, enjoying tea just like this. There was a time, a stasis, where there was real happiness here. The Box destroyed that, just like it did in all the homes around us.

"No ma, of course not. Look, I want to change things, make things better. I want to find a way to tear down the Box for good, everywhere. I don't want this suffering to keep going, generation after generation."

"All that? Do you think that's even possible then? And why can't someone else do it?"

"You know why, ma, because they won't. They haven't. It's been the same thing for centuries now. Did you know people in Sun Gate are living to nearly two centuries in age? Who's the oldest person you ever knew in the Boroughs?"

"Well your granda stayed with us till he was fifty. We used to say he was built like the city itself. Unchanging, immortal, and kind of smelly." We laugh deeply at this, and it feels so good to be with her again.

"But really now, I'm worried how dangerous this whole business is. Even when I saw you the other night, when I realized what you'd done and where you'd been. Nicholas, all I've been able to think about is wondering if you're safe."

I flinch at hearing my name again, my real name. "Ma, what I'm doing isn't safe. I'm sorry, I know you don't want to hear that, but that's the truth. Still, I have to try." I choke up a bit, and fight back the tears. "Brian saved my life last night. He sacrificed himself, took on something awful that he knew would kill him. And I can't look at that and give up on this. I won't, I'm sorry."

She nods and stares deeply into my eyes. There are tears in her eyes, too. She reaches out to grab my hand on the table. It looks different than it used to, bigger and broader, more tanned, but she holds it all the same.

"I know you won't stop, son. I knew it when I saw you that night. You've found a purpose that you have to try and fulfill, and all I can hope is that it doesn't kill you. Your da would be proud of you. He sacrificed himself to save this family, but what you're doing. Well it might save all of us."

I nod, solemnly. I hate doing this to her, but I'm so glad to get to see her. It might be the last time I do.

"Now, stop being so damn serious and tell me about this girl you're with."

I stare back at her, shocked. I hadn't mentioned Dotty at all.

"Oh come on, did you think I didn't see you two trading glances that whole night you were serving food? You think I can't tell when my own boy has fallen for someone?"

She knows me, she'll always know me, and it makes me feel at home in a way that I haven't since I left. She's artfully broken the tension that's been thick between us since I came in, and I fully relax. I spend the rest of the night telling her about my life in the clouds, and my time with Dotty. We laugh at the ridiculousness of it, and life feels easy and sweet again. Finally, as I'm nodding off at the table, she sends me to bed.

My old room is tiny to me now, the bed cramped and uncomfortable. I notice these things, but there's not a single part of me that cares. I curl onto the mattress, and it sags in the middle in the most familiar way. And as I close my eyes, I savor the sweetness of this night. Of seeing my mother again. I may never do it again, but I hope that I will. I hope one day that I can bring Dotty to meet her. And then I drift.

In the morning, I'm woken by a message on my screen. Bleary eyed, and blinking the sleep away, I look at my forearm. It's a message from Micah, and it clears every vestige of sleep from me. In an instant I'm dressed, and rushing to say bye to my mother.

Monsieur Cloudspire,

I hear you've been digging through the gutters trying to find a rat. He showed up at my doorstep, so I caught him in a trap. I've never been a fan of rodents. Please come and collect at your earliest convenience.

Your friend,

Michelangelo

CHAPTER 14

I t's so good to see Micah again that I almost forget why I'm there. We sit on his luxurious sofa over steaming cups of coffee that he's prepared. He tells me about his clients. Most of them are hilariously obsessed with some facet of their body, and it has us both in great spirits. I tell him stories of where my new life has taken me. We shed tears together over Brian's death.

"I'm concerned that there's someone involved in your story that you haven't met yet," Micah says, growing very serious suddenly.

"What do you mean?"

"I've heard of this man a few times, or the past versions of me have. I don't know much about him, but enough to steer clear. He twists and perverts things. He's like a cancer. Your survival, your rise as Allen—I'm just worried it's all a bit too perfect. Like there's an outside hand—"

"It sure hasn't felt perfect to me!" I say, but Micah's words make me think of the man that took my cancer and saved me in Brian's hospital. An ancient man in a tuxedo and top hat. I decide to not mention it in case it makes Micah worry more.

"Right, of course dear. Let's just forget I said anything. Are you ready to say hullo to this rat?"

I finish my coffee and set the cup down. "As ready as I can be."

We stand and I follow him out of the anteroom, and back towards the bedroom that I lived in during my stay. We turn before we get there though, and into a much smaller room. It's less comfortable, without the antiques or the luxurious bed. The lights are turned low, and in a chair in the corner is a man bound tightly and gagged.

"Micah, I'm surprised! How did you manage to trap him like this?"

He laughs brilliantly. "Darling, I'm a professional with anesthetics. A slight sedative in his drink, followed by a stronger dose after he went down, was enough to get him back to this room. And the ropes and gag...well I'm *very* used to using those in an entirely different setting."

I laugh deeply at this, and clap him on the back. The man in the chair wakes with the noise, and his eyes dart between the two of us. I'm still wearing blood-stained clothes, and I can see his eyes drawn to the splotches in fear.

Okay, so fear is a motivator for you. I'm tired of fear though, and I don't want to hurt you to get what I want. We'll try a new tactic here.

I step over closer to him, and the dim light in the room illuminates me better. I kneel down in front of him, and although he shies away from my face, he sees something he wasn't expecting there. Understanding, kindness, compassion.

"Here's the deal, I've been looking for you throughout Meadow Hearth because I need your help. I need armaments, expensive ones. And I need to know how to find the Plague Doctors. Against my better judgment I have a job that they'll be interested in. Now they hurt a very good friend of mine, but as long as they play nicely I'm not going to hurt them. I won't hurt you either. And if you agree to help me, I'm going to give you large sums of credits. Very, very large sums. And I think you might need that to go into hiding, am I right?

The man nods, vigorously, his eyes still wide in terror. He's a sniveling thing with dark, greasy hair that hangs down to his brown eyes. He's older, his face is lined with wrinkles, and even bound I can see the sign of a spinal deformity that must be the cause of the stoop I noticed last night. *This chair must be hell for him to sit in already.*

I reach forward and move the gag out of his mouth. Micah gives me a small glass of water, and I help the man to take a drink. He guzzles at the water greedily, and it splashes all over his face. I let him catch up on his breathing for a few moments. As he steadies himself, a businessman's keen face takes over.

"I'm sure I can sell you whatever tools you need." He smiles devilishly at this, and I suppress a shudder. *You gave weapons to monsters, and they behaved like monsters. So will I also be monstrous?* "I'm not sure I should tell you where to find the Plague Doctors though. They're a secretive bunch, and prone to retribution. I'd need assurances, a place to hide—"

I get closer to him, and bend down so we're eye to eye. I can smell the alcohol on his breath still, and I can tell my proximity has kicked off a fresh panic in him. I let my smile darken, until

I can feel the wolf beneath smiling out hungrily. From the shift on his face, he can see it too.

"Let me be clear, I have made you my kind offer. I would like to believe that kindness will be enough here, but I need your support to make that true. If things become difficult, I will make you my unkind offer. And with all the tools Micah has, it can be a *very creative* offer. Do you understand?"

He nods quickly, eager to show his understanding. This is a language he's used to, this is what he expects. The thought of torturing him makes me sick inside, and I wouldn't do it. But the bluff might be sufficient.

"Okay, I understand! Yes, I can show you where they are, and I would be happy to have your business as well. Can I ask what your intentions are?"

"No, you can't. What's your name?"

He swallows hard. "Alec Meadowhearth."

"Good, Alec, should I release you from your bonds? Please don't try to run, you won't make it far."

"Yes, sir, I won't try to run. Please release me."

I signal to Micah, and he goes around to the back of the chair and undoes the bonds. The man stretches his back gingerly and then works blood back into his wrists. He looks at me, and there's no malice in his gaze, but a mild surprise. I'm sure he didn't expect to be released without some new pain being applied.

"Let's discuss armaments first, Alec. Will you lead me to your shop?"

"Yes sir, of course. But if any of the Doctors see me leading you, they may expect deceit."

"I'll call a driver, I have one I trust for their discretion," Micah says as he leaves the room.

I stare Alec in the eyes, unblinking, until he looks away.

"Don't cross me, Alec. Someone I love died because of weapons you sold, and I'm trying to be a better man for him. But vengeance still appeals to me."

Alec nods and stares at the floor, refusing to meet my gaze.

The driver Micah calls wears a mask when he arrives, an opaque thing that distorts and shifts his face underneath, and never speaks a word. Alec tells him where his shop is, and the driver wordlessly carries us there. Once we've left the tram, he leaves. I'm alone with Alec in a quiet hole of Meadow Hearth. It's one of the few residential sections, nestled in the alleys between shop fronts. He leads me to an abandoned building with a crumbling stone facade. A short set of stairs leads up to where a door once stood. It's now an open maw into a dark void.

I follow him in, stepping carefully over debris so as to not call attention to us. We enter the home, go down a stairwell and turn right. Once we're entirely out of sight, Alec touches his hand to his temple and a small light ring illuminates around his eyes. I've never seen the tech before, not many have the money or desire for mods like this. He leads me over more rubble to a locked metal door.

In the shining light, fresh oil glistens on the hinges. He touches his hand to the door, and the biolock releases with a quiet *click*. I follow him inside and into blackness, and as the door latches shut behind us, lights turn on all around us. For a brief moment, I'm blinded and wondering if this is a trap of his own, but as my eyes adjust I see that he's been true to his word. The walls and display cases around the room are brimming with armaments.

He taps his temples again to turn off his eye lights. "I'm sorry that the Doctors killed someone you loved. I really, well I never thought they'd do what they did."

"Did you think they were buying those weapons for no reason?"

"To be honest, I never sold that much to them. A few sets of breathing apparatuses, a handful of plasma blades, but no big tech. They couldn't afford that stuff. It was all fine until they got their new chemist on board—" he says it, and something the Doctors said at that party flashes back to me. *A real curious thing our lab rats built,* that man had said.

"Who was their chemist then? The one that supplied them with plague?" I ask.

"Came from up top, real high up. But they wouldn't tell me any more than that. Nasty stuff they brought, I heard what happened at that party." He turns and stares at my uniform. "I'm guessing you were there, then?"

I nod, and he shakes his head. "They're a bunch of idiots really, they don't even know what they want. They're just angry and want to make people hurt the way they hurt."

There's an understanding in his words. I see it too, they're no different from who I used to be. They're willing to sacrifice others to get the change they want, they think the rich are all evil, they want to see them hurt. But I found humanity on my path here, and they may have lost theirs entirely. *They've killed so many already, I don't know if I can change them. If they can only be monsters, I may have to destroy them.*

"I'm not here to debate their morals, I just want to know where they are, Alec."

He stares into my face for a while before he responds. The fear from earlier seems to have faded. "I understand. Let me show you my wares, then!"

He pivots and makes a grand sweeping gesture with his arm. The walls are lined with weapons and tools of all sorts. There are grappling devices like the Centurions used, an entire wall of plasma blades, and as I approach the main counter, I see a melter sitting in a transparent display case. It's small, a one handed operation, but the barrel is nearly the length of my forearm and it has a scope on top. I've never seen one in person, there are barely even photos of them.

He sees where my eyes are looking, and laughs. "That's my prize piece there. You know not even Inquisitors and Centurions are allowed to carry that tech, it's too big of a risk that it will damage the city. I got it from someone whose family smuggled it in, centuries ago."

"And it still works?" I say, not taking my eyes off the thing.

"Aye, they don't really go bad. Draws its charge from the air, but it takes time. Thing like that, it might only squeeze a shot a minute. Not great for rush jobs. Long barrel and scope shows it's more meant for distance and accuracy. Any idea what you might be interested in? What's your budget?"

I pull my eyes away, and realize I haven't even thought about it. *The kind of credits I'd spend here would almost certainly get my account locked down, so I need to be damn sure what I'm buying.* "I need something for defense, and something to handle Inquisitors too. I might want that melter, but I'm not certain." His eyes widen and look like they'll pop out of his skull. I'm not sure if it's at the mention of me going up against Inquisitors, or at the amount of money he might get from me.

Alec turns around, and beckons me to follow. He takes me to a back room, basically an attached supply closet, and turns over a tarp on the ground. Underneath it is a huge mass of shimmering black. He stands back, letting me inspect, so I move closer. It's hard to tell the shape, so I poke it with my finger. It feels warm, alive. As I'm watching, the shape morphs.

The indistinguishable mass was a pile of multiple sleeves and pants fit for a giant. They shrink down to a size that would fit me. The length seems tailor made, and two of the arms neatly disappear. Before me now are two identical body suits of beautiful, shimmering black.

"It's cosmic armor, at least that's what they call it. Same thing Centurions wear from what I've heard, but thankfully I've never seen them in person. It's self-healing, fits itself to each user as you just saw, and will stop most blades and projectiles."

I recognize it as the armor I saw slow down a plasma blade, which is seriously impressive. "Will it stop a melter?"

"Depending on the range and intensity, maybe. A close up shot would still fry you though. I certainly wouldn't count on it."

"I'll take both of them, now what about something against Inquisitors?"

"We haven't even discussed cost?"

"That's fine, we can at the end."

Alec closes his gaping mouth, and turns out of the supply closet, beckoning me to follow him. Back in the main room, underneath the wall of plasma blades, he shows me what look like a pair of brass knuckles, but in the palm support is a thumb-sized cylinder. There's a tiny green light on each of them.

He turns back to me, a showman's smile on his face. "These are EMP fists, they release a tiny electromagnetic pulse into anything they hit. Inquisitors are internally protected from long-range EMP, but something this close will definitely shut them down. Just like the melter, these things have limited charges, but they'll recharge over time. That's not the real limiter though."

"And what is, then?"

"They get hot. Really, really hot. More than a couple of uses in a short time period will make them hot enough to burn, more than that might melt skin. As I understand it, these only ever made it to the prototyping phase. Their use was too limited."

I nod, thinking it over. "Okay, I'll take it all. The armor, the melter, these knuckles, and I want one of those plasma blades too. My knife is useful, but a bit short. What's the cost?"

Alec's visibly sweating. He walks back to his counter and starts going through files, pulling out sheaths of crumpled paper and writing figures down on a piece of paper. He stares at it for a while, his pen stuck in his mouth, and then puts the piece of paper in front of me.

I laugh, maniacally. It's an astronomical sum, a quarter of the family wealth of Allen Cloudspire that I have access to. A part of me feels shame at the thought of stealing from this dead man's family, but there is no other course open to me. *I'll consider it reparations, then.*

"If I pay this, they will shut down my account. They will track this location, probably nearly immediately. You will have to leave this place."

It's Alec's turn to laugh, his whole body shaking. "Look, if you pay for all this I don't have much of value left to sell. It's more money than I could dream of. If you pay this I'm packing up and going deep into hiding."

I nod, thinking it over. "Can we time-delay the transfer one day? That will give us both some time to evacuate."

He nods. "Those are acceptable terms to me."

I queue up the credits on my screen, and show it to him for approval. His eyes are massive, and his mouth is hanging open, but he nods still. *I will no longer be welcome as Allen Cloudspire. This is a bridge I can't repair.* I set the transfer back one day, and hold my arm out. He eagerly grabs it with his own forearm, and the deed is done.

Alec helps me to put on the gear. The cosmic armor morphs over me like a second skin, it's incredibly light and barely hinders movement. I put it on under my clothes, and in the mirror you can't even see it. The melter I strap in a holster at my hip, and the plasma blade right next to it. I have no way to conceal them from sight, so I'll have to try to not attract any attention on the street. The knuckles go into the front pockets of my uniform.

I feel ridiculous, shit, I *look* ridiculous in all of this. I barely know how half of it works, although Alec shows me all the different buttons and things to know. I try to copy his words verbatim to memory, and touch the different toggles and switches in my hand to memorize their feel. He wraps the second suit of cosmic armor behind paper. It looks like a present when he's done, which will do perfectly.

As a gift, Alec throws in a tracker ball. It's a neat bit of tech, any place that the user thinks of it can map to, but they have to have been there before and seen the way. He holds it to his temple and it programs with the location of the Plague Doctors. Or at least, I hope that's where it's sending us.

"The way there gets a little *wet*. All of your gear is fine for that. You could use a shower anyways," he adds, laughing. My purchases seem to have made him forgive me for the threats earlier. "You'll be going down into the sewers. Follow the walk down from the Metal Oyster to the bottom of the Boroughs. You'll find a maintenance access door there. Oh, and before I forget. You'll want these." He reaches under the counter, and pulls out a handful of cotton balls. He motions them going up his nose, and then hands them over to me. "It gets pretty bad at times down there."

I stuff them in my pocket, and take a few deep breaths to calm my nerves. Then I pen a message on my screen, and send it off.

Hullo Dotty,

How does a night out at the Metal Oyster sound? I'll see you there at sunset.

Entirely Yours,

Allen Cloudspire

Everything is in motion now, time to find out where this road ends.

CHAPTER 15

From the light on the walk, I can only make out the line of Dotty's neck as she stands in the shadows of an alley behind the Oyster. I've given her the wrapped parcel from Alec, and explained what it is. She's brought a pair of black waterproof tights and jacket that will cover the armor perfectly. She even managed to get a similar set of clothes for me when she went to my house, and I'm eternally grateful to remove the blood and puke stained uniform. I can't believe it's only been two days since that party at the Skyball. Time has stretched and expanded too much since then.

Charon sits at my side in the shadows. I'm absent mindedly scratching his chin, and he's giving a deeply gratifying purr. He's the real reason I asked her to stop there. I've grown fond of the panther, and Dotty gave him the choice of staying in Cloudspire or coming with us. He'd been sleeping on my bed still, and only responded with a hissed, *"So he's alive"* as he followed her stealthily back out of the house.

Dotty finishes changing and walks back out of the alley, giving me a small nod to show that she's ready. There's a satchel on her back. She told me only that it contains something of her father's that will let us through the biometric lock. I decided not to pursue it further, hoping instead that it wasn't too gruesome. The three of us make our way down the walk, keeping to the shadows and avoiding any crowds we see. There are a few tense moments in Meadow Hearth where we have to duck into an alley to avoid some drunks, but by the time we reach Five Boroughs the streets are empty. We move quickly then, making our way further and further down to the sewers.

We stop within sight of the maintenance access to shove cotton into our nostrils. The stench is so overwhelming already it's making me nauseous. The cotton dulls the smell, but also makes it feel like it's stuck inside my nose. I focus on movement, and try to ignore the stench.

The access door is small and round, with a large turn lock. I grab it firmly, expecting resistance, but it turns easily and swings open. The three of us move into the darkness beyond. From the glow of the street lamps, we can see that we're on a low-ceiling walkway that sits barely above the steady stream of sewage. The smell is other-worldly, and as soon as we move inside, Dotty leans against the wall and vomits. I follow up right behind her.

I close the door, and we're left in pure darkness. It's eerie knowing Dotty and Charon are right beside me, but feeling like I'm alone in the universe. I blindly find the tracker ball in my pocket, and when I depress the button on top it shoots into the air. A mesh of white light scans our surroundings. The suddenly intense light in the otherwise pitch blackness blinds us momentarily, and we all turn our faces from it. The tracker then beeps smartly, and starts to move down the corridor.

It always stays the same distance ahead. Close enough to add some light, but far enough that large stretches of the walk are still covered in darkness. We make our way slowly at first, but as we get more comfortable with our surroundings the pace increases. All three of us are moving as noiselessly as possible, afraid to wake anything that might be down here. My brain makes monsters of the darkness, of every sound, but I focus on movement and it helps to keep my nerves somewhat calm.

The sewers seem to be an endless series of passageways. Since we entered, they've branched in so many directions that I wouldn't be able to find my way back. We're dependent on this tracker, and I nervously realize what a mistake that might have been. Alec could have easily programmed it to put us in the center of this maze, knowing that we'd die before we got back out.

What can we do, but follow it now? I don't have another option.

The smell has changed since we entered, or I've gotten used to it. I motion to Dotty to stop, and pull the cotton from my nose. The smell of the sewers is a distant memory, barely lingering around the edges of the humid air. The rush of water hasn't changed next to us, but now it smells fresh. I bend down and cup some in my hand, and after smelling it up close, hesitantly put it to my lips. I taste clean, crisp water.

Up to this point I hadn't considered the distribution of clean water through the city. There's no naturally occurring springs here. If refuse flows from everywhere down to the Boroughs, clean water must flow from here out to the city. If these tunnels follow that water, then they'd allow access to every part of the city. I'm starting to see how the Plague Doctors have operated without the Inquisitors being aware.

When I stand back up, I realize we've lost sight of the tracker around a corner. The three of us pick up our pace to get it back in eyesight. We round the corner, and step right off the edge of the walkway.

I see the walkway continues straight above us as we spiral into the blackness. It fades from view as we suddenly fall down a steep, round chute. Covered in water, the three of us are a jumbled mess of limbs. We're all trying to arrest ourselves against the wall, but it's counterproductive. I grab for the wall and accidentally punch Dotty in the face, while she knees me in the groin trying to stop her foot on something. Charon tries to jump off of me to safety, but just hits the wall. And just as falling starts to feel normal, the chute disappears entirely, and we're spat into a brightly illuminated room.

I'm really falling now, end over end, in the tumultuous flow of a waterfall. I can only hope that there's water in the landing. I'm blind from the sudden light, and flipping around too much to get any bearings. I splash down into a deep pool, but I only feel thankful for the soft landing for a moment. Slick flesh writhes all around me. Massive, wet bodies are hitting me all over, and I almost pull out my plasma knife to fight back. But without being able to see, I might hurt Dotty or Charon, and it's a risk I can't take. I open my eyes, and swim toward the light. My vision is obscured by the writhing forms that constantly career into my legs, arms, and face. I fight against it for the surface.

As I breach, I see Dotty off to my left, splashing chaotically. The water is alive and turbulent all around us. Something is trying to drown us, smother us, and I can't let it end like this. And then, a large trout hops out of the water right in front of me, and it breaks through my fear.

"They're just fish! Holy shit, they're just fish!"

"WHAT?!" Dotty yells back, barely staying afloat.

Calm now, I swim through the writhing mass towards her, and keep her afloat. I'm laughing hysterically now.

"They're just fish! I thought we were going to die, but they're just fucking fish!"

Her face is as dumbstruck as I feel. We laugh together in the water, like we've conquered death. As we stop moving, the waters slowly calm. We're in a high-ceilinged rectangular room. There's a walkway that rings this pool and several doors split off from it. Charon surfaces near the walkway and pulls himself onto it. He has a fish in his jaws, and is already setting into it.

We swim toward him, and pull ourselves out of the water. Thankfully, this was all clean water we were in, and I shudder to think if it had been sewage instead.

A small metal oyster sign hangs above one of the doors, and I point it out to Dotty. "I guess that explains where their fish come from," I say, and we grin at each other for finding the solution to such an old mystery.

We sit on the edge for some time, watching the fish swim. The pool of water is completely full of them, a mass of different colors and sizes. *Born in a metal box, just waiting to be chosen for slaughter. Waiting for someone wealthy to decide to eat them.* Charon has finished his meal, and is drinking from the pool.

Calm now, I notice the tracker is dutifully waiting at a door opposite of the entrance to the Metal Oyster. We slowly gather ourselves, and continue to follow it.

The path here is taller and well lit, but no less confusing. We follow the tracker through meandering corridors and countless forks. There are more pools of fish on the way, they're smaller the further we get from the main room. These must be the hatcheries then. There are signs labeling them. *Rainbow trout, Chilean sea bass, Atlantic salmon*. Some of the words are strange to me, foreign. We see several signs pointing towards the *bluefin tuna* pool, but the tracker takes us in a different direction.

After what feels like miles, we round a corner and find the tracker stopped in front of a door. There's graffiti all over it, from obscene images to sayings like *Eat The Rich* and *Chaos is a Lifestyle*. The tracker beeps again, and when I hold out my hand, the tracker returns to it and turns off. The three of us stare at the door for a while. I can tell that Dotty is really nervous, she's breathing hard and erratically.

I find her hand, and squeeze it. "It's going to be fine, I'll go in first and Charon after me. We're just here to talk with them." There are tears in her eyes for some reason, and she's gone very pale. She nods meekly, and I turn back toward the door.

I pull out my new melter. It may not be the right tool against a group of people, but it sure looks like it would dissuade conflict. I take a deep breath, and then throw the door open. It slams against the inside wall, and I rush in with Charon at my heels and my melter held high.

The inside of the room is bigger than I could have ever anticipated. After the claustrophobic tunnels it feels entirely out of place. There are around twenty men and women scattered through the room, and they all turn to stare at the noise. Some of them were playing cards at a small table, others were over relaxing on the cots in the corner. Some are working in a kitchen that completely lines the far wall, the food smells rich and delicious. Corridors continue out the back of the room, and a few faces have appeared out of them already. I'm briefly stunned by the scale of it—it's so much more than I imagined.

"Well hullo there monsters, we're here to recruit you!" I yell out from the doorway. I try my best for bravado, even if we're drastically outnumbered.

The four that were playing cards stand and draw out plasma blades, and others in the room scurry for weapons. But then when Dotty enters the room behind me, their whole gravity switches to her. They relax, and put away their weapons. I'm surprised, but not disappointed. And as I'm starting to turn back to her to say something, I feel something sharp slam into the base of my neck.

A cold fire spreads through my body, and I twist to see Dotty holding a syringe in both me and Charon. I try to speak, but my tongue is feeling heavy. I lock eyes with her, they're heavy and sad, full of internal grief. Charon and I both fall to our knees at the same time. *Why, Dotty? I thought you were the one I could trust.* Darkness slams into me as I collapse on the floor.

I wake as my conscious brain tries to free itself from the tranquilizer. Charon and I lay on a cot together, both of us bound so we can't move. There's a gag over my mouth. Everything around me is swimming, so I keep my eyes closed and listen. And think.

I see the pattern, obvious now on the other side of knowledge. Voices echo inside my skull like a warning that I didn't pay attention to. *It was all fine until they got their new chemist...Came from up top, real high up,* I hear Alec saying, and I hear Dotty responding, *I don't know how we tear it down. It all has to change.*

Why didn't I think she was capable of doing this? She's been working on this for longer than I have, and she's been stymied for years. Living in Sun Gate, she'd have seen no other way to change it.

It tears me apart inside. Not just the betrayal, but thinking of her choosing to kill all those people. *It was a party of nearly all politicals, isn't that the perfect target if you want to change the government?* I see the concern on her face when she saw me there, how she drew me away from the main level where the gas would hit first, how she turned on her gas mask instantly and yelled at me to do the same. It breaks my heart. All those people, dead.

I hear myself telling Brian, *the end justifies these means,* and realize she has been saying the same thing this entire time. Thinking of Brian turns a knife in my guts. *Brian is dead because of the gas she gave to these monsters. Because of the attack she planned with them.* And with that thought the tears come freely.

Someone sits down on the edge of the bed, and I know her smell. I open my eyes to see her face swimming across my vision.

I can tell she's hurting too, she reaches out and brushes the hair back behind my ear. She's tender, and loving, and I just want to return to a world where that's all there is between us.

"I'm sorry, Allen. If I should even call you that. I'm still not sure what your real name is." Cold fear grips me at that, adrenaline courses through me and crystallizes my focus. "Oh yes, I've known you weren't him since you came back. I took a bit of your hair at the party that first night to analyze. But you see, I needed someone to help me. Someone from either Cloud Spire or Sun Gate has to do it, it won't work for anyone else. Since your DNA was altered, it should respond to you."

What is she talking about? What does she need me for?

"I've had this vision for *so long*, but I could never convince Allen. He wasn't even interested in politics, and the harder I'd push the more he'd drift away. You showed me that first night that you cared deeply, you wanted to change things.

"And the deeper I looked, the more I loved what I saw. You're this kind, caring man who just wanted to save the world. It makes my heart ache to look at you now, tied down and drugged. In a different universe, none of this was necessary. I know I'll feel shame for it for the rest of my life. But we have to end this thing, and I know you agree with that. I'm sorry. If it's any consolation, I do love you." She bends down and kisses me on the temple, and then she tenderly slides another needle between my knuckles. With a lurch, reality dissolves, and I drift again.

Chapter 16

When I come to, we're moving down a corridor. I'm still in a cot with Charon, but we're floating now at waist height. There's a mass of people around us. As my vision starts to clear, I see they're all wearing Plague Doctor disguises. All of them except for Dotty. She's next to my cot, marching with her eyes facing forward. The melter and plasma blade I bought are strapped to her hip, so close I could reach out and grab them. I'm still bound though, and there's no way I could fight off this many people anyway.

Sleep tugs at me still, but I try to focus on the conversation around me. I try to absorb.

"That's the core down that way. Whole city is tied into that thing, take it out and all the lights go out. One of these days we'll hit that, show those rich cats real power." The voice is high, and I can hear the sneer in its tone.

"You fucking moron, that would probably kill everyone, including us."

"Only if the outside isn't livable, but I've heard there's data to support—"

"You've heard damn rumors, no one could know that."

"Well either way. If we died too at least we'd take them with us."

"Aye, or what if instead we attacked the water supply with plague? I bet we'd take out a fair sort before anyone realized."

Fear grips me at the mention of plague. *They are monsters, there isn't a way for them to live in this world. How is Dotty not putting a stop to this horrific dreaming?* I look at her face, and I can see the disgust clearly, even in profile. *A means to an end, then. If I get a chance to stop them, I have to take it.*

"Squash it, we have the mission to talk over. Is everyone crystal on what to do when Miss Sungate opens the door?"

"We sneak in all quiet-like and gas the Centurions where they sleep," several people say this simultaneously, reciting an earlier command.

"Aye, their barracks are right inside the door and we don't really want them coming to join the party. So we'll plant a few and close em in, clear? And by quiet-like, I mean like the dead, no fucking chit-chat after that door opens."

"Clear, boss."

"Meanwhile, Dorothy is going to the control room to use her daddy's key to unlock our path to the top. We rendezvous on the top floor to deal with Cerberus."

Cerberus? What is—

"Kinda hot of you to be carrying around a detached hand, *Miss Sungate,*" the one with the sneer in his voice says to Dorothy.

With practiced ease she swirls around, grabs the plasma blade from her belt, and extends the blade outwards. From the back, I watch her pin someone against the wall with the point of it in one fluid motion. Her movements are practiced, and executed so quickly I barely keep up. The mass of people pauses to watch, but I don't think anyone is about to interfere.

"Keep your mouth shut or I take your tongue out, you fucking snake. I didn't enjoy taking it from him, but from you I'll take a real pleasure."

She took her father's hand?!

"Aye miss, sorry miss. Crystal clear."

She stows the blade away again, and the contingent starts moving.

The conversation dies, and as much as I try to stay awake, drugged sleep rides my shoulders and pulls at my eyelids. I drift off again.

I float back to reality when we pause at a gigantic golden wall. There's a pedestal on the right side, but no obvious way forward. For the first time since I went to Sun Gate, I can feel the wings on my back wake up. I had forgotten they were there still, and apparently so has Dotty. I'm careful to not move at all though, and I keep my eyes mostly closed as I try to watch what's happening.

So we're inside the gates now, but still underground. Is this golden wall the entrance to the Medical Authority then?

The Plague Doctors have organized in a two-by-two line, and I float in my cot on their left. I can barely make out Dotty on the other side of the column. She's standing in front of the pedestal. I watch as she reaches into her jacket, and pulls out *a hand*. Even from here I can see it's sealed in some transparent wrapping. She carefully unwraps it and places it on the pedestal. From where I lay, I just catch sight of dried blood smeared on cold flesh. A chill races down my spine.

A shimmering, electric hum fills the room. *The sound of hidden machinery.* I rotate my head slightly and watch the golden wall. A slight wave of vibration travels from the floor to the ceiling, and then the metal wall pulls open like a stage curtain. It folds and bunches without seams until it reaches the ceiling, and then it disappears into it. Behind it is a gaping, dimly lit hallway that disappears out of my sight range.

Tall enough for Centurions, I think, and barely stifle a shudder.

The people in the column stare at the sight with as much wonder as I feel. Someone at the front separates from formation, and facing the column, starts to direct with hand signals. Then they march silently into the building as I float alongside. I can just see Dotty at the front of the column, her eyes leveled forward.

We creep inside for some time like this. The hallway is slightly curved, and seems to be tightening as we continue. Eventually we reach an end, and there's a gigantic door on each side. One has a pedestal, and for the other there's a complex computer screen. The screen is dark, with no obvious sign of life. There's whispering at the front, and I can just barely make it out.

"Control room...to unlock"
"Open...Centurion barracks"
"Rendezvous...elevator"

Through the crowd I watch Dotty approach the pedestal and set something on it. The doorway near it slides up into the ceiling and reveals a grand elevator behind. She steps onto it, and the door slides shut. The Plague Doctors seem to be preparing for battle. I watch as those around me reposition plasma blades on their hips, and count their gas canisters. There's a nervous energy in the air, a palpable tension.

I take the time to assess my own situation as well. My hands and feet are bound, but I think my wings might be free. I shift slightly and feel the EMP knuckles against my thigh, and joy washes over me. *I never told Dotty about those, they're still in my pocket!* With focus, I can just feel the hidden plasma knife that Micah gave me. As I'm shifting around, I lock eyes with Charon. He's awake too now, but also being silent and still. I wink at him, and I swear he smiles back.

There's a plan forming in my mind, but I don't know what situation I'll be in yet. *Surely they won't take us inside the barracks with them? Will they leave a guard with us?*

Dotty must have made it to the control room, in a flash the computer panel in front of the other door lights up. The Doctors form in their double column, facing the door, but I'm left against the far wall. One of them stands in front of the door, hand poised on top of a gigantic red button on the screen. A man I think, by his stature, but the uniforms make it difficult to tell. He presses it, and the door slides open. The darkness inside is complete, but a harmony of rumblings fills the air.

Is that snoring? Are those monsters snoring?

The line creeps in, silently. They all disappear inside, except for the one at the switch panel. I steel myself, counting the seconds and imagining the distance the column has covered inside. *I need them to be far enough away, but I can't wait too long.*

My whole body is in tension as I think through what I have to execute. I visualize each muscle twitch, each momentary goal, and then I open my eyes and stare at the Doctor left by the panel. Noiselessly, I spring my plasma knife. As it slides out, it cuts the bonds on my hands. Free now, I move one quickly into my jacket pocket, and slide my left hand through one of the EMP knuckles.

What happens next has to be swift and merciless, there's no room for error. I focus on my rage, and my pain, and it makes my nerves like iron. I know I can't let these monsters live, any of them. They'll just keep causing pain and destruction, it's all they know. It's all they want. More attacks like the party, or worse. It ends here.

In one swift motion, I pull open my wings and rise out of the cot. The Plague Doctor sees me, and starts to reach for his plasma blade. *Too slow.* I use all the speed of my wings, and barrel at him, my knife leading in front of me. In a split second, I've buried it through his mask and into his skull, right where his eye should be. My energy carries us forward, and slams him into the wall. Noise echoes around us, through the hallway and into the darkness of the room. My nose is full of the smell of burning flesh as the blue knife continuously burns and cauterizes the wound, and I flex my wrist to pull it back. The Doctor slumps to the floor, blood spilling from the hole I made.

In the darkness inside that room, things are stirring that defy reality. Great, nightmarish things. I pull back my left fist now, and slam the knuckles into the switch by the door. The circuits fry instantly as a small EMP pulse detonates inside them, and smoke billows up from the panel as the door slides noiselessly shut. Not a single Doctor makes it out.

I'm a good man, but there is a need for vengeance here that overpowers any sense of decency. *I need to know they're dead. I need to bury them and know they won't be back.* Without a hint of mercy, I pound my fist on the door as hard as I can. It echoes inside the cavernous room, and then the movement of the brutes behind it causes quakes through the floor.

Sounds are muffled from the door between us, but I hear enough. What starts with yelled orders from the Plague Doctors, quickly turns into screams of pain. There's the faint hissing of gas inside the room, followed by the giant impact of Centurions hitting the ground after succumbing to it. But over the top of it, there are more and more screams from the Doctors. I imagine the carnage in that room, and shudder. I stand there, and wait until the screams stop. Centurions continue to collapse from the gas for several more minutes, but then that stops too. *It's done, the thing is done. There was no place for any of them in this world.*

I bend down and cut the bonds at my feet now. I've never intentionally killed anyone before this, and I tell myself I should feel shaken. Instead, I feel numb and full of a cold purpose. I've made it inside the facility, I'm free from my captors, and I have a few weapons still. Using my knife, I carve an inscription in the door.

Here there be monsters. I hope no one ever opens the door.

I walk back to the cot, where Charon has been noiselessly watching me, and cut his bonds. He jumps down from the cot and stretches his back, and then sits down to lick his paws. He is unphased by the violence.

"Let's go see what's at the top of this thing, eh boy?"

He nods slightly, and plods along behind me as I go to the elevator. Lights dance over the pedestal in front, and I press the only button on it. The door to the massive elevator hisses open, and we step inside. There are no buttons inside, but as soon as I think *"top floor"* the elevator slides into motion. It accelerates quickly, and then I'm left in stasis as we rocket upwards. A soft chime fills the space with each level we pass.

The elevator comes to a stop so abruptly that both Charon and I are launched into the air, and come crashing down in a heap. There's nothing in here to tell me what floor we're on. I can faintly hear a chittering, metal on metal sound outside the door. It's like some giant mechanical thing with several legs is moving across the floor. *Inquisitors. Shit. They must have realized the intrusion.*

I reach into my jacket and wrap each of my hands through one of the EMP knuckles. The one I used downstairs has long since cooled, but I remember what Alec told me. There's only so many uses I get before these things melt my hands off. The chittering has drawn nearer to the elevator door, and I can feel it resonating through the floors now. I ready myself for what comes next, I'll have to move quickly and—

The access door in the ceiling of the elevator suddenly blows open, and an Inquisitor lands at my side. I go to hit him, but the spindly mechanical thing is much, much faster. The knife-like fingers from its right hand shoot towards me. I'm way too slow to dodge. They hit me in the chest, and I brace for the oncoming pain.

But it never comes. I open my eyes, realizing that I've squeezed them shut out of fear, and see the Inquisitor's fingers have barely marked my armor. The energy from the blow that likely should have impaled me, or sent me flying, has been redirected back up through the hand. It crumbles and shatters, a broken thing. There's a small amount of heat at the impact site, but nothing else. Both the Inquisitor and I are staring at it, and realization hits us together. I started swinging my fist when the thing landed, and like a gag punch it strikes the Inquisitor then. My hand connects with that faceless mask, a tiny EMP launching through the mechanical brain inside. Plumes of smoke pour from it.

The Inquisitor falls in on itself, no longer held up by the intricate processors and machinery that defined its existence. It all happens in the span of a moment, but there's no time to stop and think. The elevator door slides open, and I see ten more of the mechanical monsters crawl over the walls towards me. They're down on all fours, launching themselves across the broad hallway. Charon and I pile out of the elevator, running headlong towards them.

When the first one springs for me, Charon has already anticipated it. He bowls into its side, upsetting its balance enough that I easily connect a punch. It falls, and the other Inquisitors pause momentarily. *Holy fuck, are they learning?* It's all the time I get to think before two more launch from the walls towards us. This time, one is aimed right for Charon. I intercept, diving in front of Charon and letting the Inquisitor pile into me. It shatters up past the arms, and I tap it on the head with my knuckles.

Charon launches at another behind me now, sending an attack aimed at my head squarely over my shoulder. *My head is not armored, if they hit me, they'll take it clean off.* I whirl around and catch it near the jaw. The knuckles are starting to get hot now, they're warm against my hands. The Inquisitors pause again, and I look down the hall for escape. A spiraling staircase leads upwards at the end of the hallway. The metal railing on the outside might offer some small protection. I run for it.

The next hits me on my right side. Instead of trying to knock me down, he grapples with my right hand to try and pry one of the knuckles from me. I hit him with my left hand moments before another one of them tries to do the same on that side. *Their timing was just a split second off, otherwise they might have snared me.* My right hand free now, I hit the one on the left, and then keep running. My hands are burning now, I want to drop the fists but they're the only way I can survive this.

Two more land in front of me, blocking my entrance to the staircase. I don't even slow down—I lunge forward with hands outstretched, my wings springing open to propel me. My fists tag each of them as I pile onto the stairs, and the adrenaline and pain forces me to my feet again. I can't look down, but I can feel my hands blistering underneath the knuckles. Everything in me wants to drop them, but I hold on and focus on running up the stairs.

It's a tight spiral, and I gain elevation quickly. All around me there's skittering as more Inquisitors climb the stairs and up the railings all around me. I focus on the top, where a door splits the ceiling. *That better be unlocked or I'm fucked.* My breathing is coming in ragged gasps, but I've trained my running for weeks now and I can bear the pain.

An Inquisitor grabs me over the railing on my right, trying to pull me over with him, but my left fist darts out and knocks him down. Blood splatters on his face, my own blood. I catch sight of my hand for a second, and it's gruesome. I ignore it, I ignore the pain, I ignore everything else but the running. I get to the door at the top, and rush towards it. It slides open just before impact, and when I've made it through I see a manual control panel on my right. I punch it without thinking, frying the mechanism, and drop the knuckles from both of my hands.

I'm uncontrollably sobbing in pain. My hands are a mess of blisters and blood. Flesh is melted so far that I can see muscle on my right hand. Exposed to the air now, all of the pain floods my nerve receptors and I start to black out. Then I hear her voice.

"Did you just seal that door?! FUCK, that was our way out!"

I turn to see Dotty, blood trickling down her face from a cut at her temple. She's lit from the back, and for a moment all I can think is how beautiful she is like this. Fighter, leader, giver, lover, human. And then I see the monster behind her, and time stops.

Chapter 17

Dotty grabs my arm, and we fly into the air. Away from the great beast. The thing that's broken my reality so that all I can do is stare back at it while we try to get distance. The room we're in is cavernous. A dome that's easily fifty feet tall in the center and three hundred feet wide. With arms extended, this monster could still reach the ceiling. It makes Centurions look like playthings, and us like insects.

Like the Centurions, there are features of it that look vaguely human. It's supported on giant legs like tree trunks, but there are four of them. Each is shaped somewhat differently, like they were hastily modeled out of clay. It causes the beast to lean to one side, but doesn't seem to slow it down as it *scurries* across the floor after us. A giant, meaty torso sits on top, with four arms that hang and extend nearly to the floor.

But the thing that I can't stop staring at are the *heads*. As in, more than one. Two fearsome heads sit on top of the shoulders. Their jaws are extended outwards absurdly, with seemingly endless rows of sharp teeth lining them and sticking out in all directions. The hateful yellow eyes are narrowed into slits as it chases us. The drool dripping from its mouth sends a shudder down my spine. They're both different sizes, with different bone structures, but they look like they could have been based on a human's head.

I finally come to my senses enough to yell at Dorothy, "What the fuck is that thing?!"

She looks back at me briefly, tenderly, and then pulls her eyes forward. "That's Cerberus, named after the dog that guarded the gates of hell. It was an early attempt at facemelting two people together. When it went horribly wrong, the doctors involved decided they should just continue making it a monster. It was the prototype for the Centurions that were made later. My father told me the story when I was young."

"They intentionally made that thing?! For what purpose?"

"To guard the door we need to get through. It won't open as long as that thing has a pulse."

I stare back at it again, and see the misshapen limbs again. *Different from each other because they were once different people.* We're flying in a circular path around the dome, and it's dutifully chasing us. There is no getting distance from the beast, we're just biding time.

"The facemelting tech that made you someone else, this is its root. This is where it originated."

I shudder at that, seeing the great thing that paved the way for me to become Allen. It's horrifying.

"Okay, so what's your plan here? Surely you had a plan when you came here?"

"I *planned* to have the Plague Doctors fight it. But with you here by yourself, I'm guessing that's no longer a viable option? The plan was to wait for them in the room below, but I was stormed by Inquisitors and had to run."

"The Plague Doctors won't be coming here. I can't believe you worked with those monsters."

"Not the time for that discussion, Allen!" she says admonishingly as we dodge lower in elevation. The huge beast had lunged for us, one of its arms scraping the air right where we were moments earlier.

I reach down and grab the melter off her waist. "Well, if I remember correctly, we fly faster alone." I bring my feet up and kick off of her, sending us both flying in opposite directions. The great thing behind us hesitates, seeing us split off. One head tracks each of us, but it can't choose.

"Don't miss, you could put a hole in the city with that damn thing!" she screams after me.

If I can't miss, then I need to be close.

I fly up above the thing, and then drop my wings and use them to propel me toward it. The arms come for me immediately, but I close my eyes and let the wings tell me how to move through it. Momentarily clear of them, I open my eyes and find I'm right next to the heads. The stench is unreal, rotting food hangs from the teeth, some remnant of an earlier meal. I level the melter at the head nearest me, and squeeze the trigger. Pain lances through my hand with the pressure.

A red line of energy shoots from the barrel. It travels through the air in an impossibly straight line, and tunnels a hole straight through the forehead of one of the beasts. The skin around the hole melts and dissolves, and for a moment I pause in flight to watch it. It's incredible to see the hole grow as everything around it turns black, and disappears into the air. I realize my mistake only when one of the massive hands grabs me out of the air, knocking the melter from my hand and the air from my lungs. The gun smashes against the ground far beneath me, probably broken.

Cerberus is howling in pain, dancing around and swinging me through the air. From my new prison I watch as one of its heads continue to evaporate until only the lower jaw is left protruding from a blackened neck. It fights through the pain, focuses its hateful eyes back on me, and squeezes.

I brace for it, thinking my head might explode off my body with the pressure from it, but my suit helps protect me. The thing's muscles strain against it, and I feel an immense pressure all around me. It hurts like hell, and my hands pulsate painfully as fresh bloods oozes from them, but I won't die. I can see the frustration on its face as it tries and tries to squeeze the life out of me. Then it decides to take a new approach.

Another one of the hands comes up to grab my arms. *Oh fuck, it's going to pull me apart.* This is definitely not how I'd like to die, but it turns out I don't get a say in it. It grabs each arm, and pulls. The pain is immense, and I tense all of my muscles against it. I summon all the strength I've built training to pull my arms together, the whole of my world distilling to electro-chemical signals sent from my brain that tell my muscles to contract. I hear the brute straining against me, but it isn't enough. The suit holds me together, barely, and from the corner of my eye I can see a seam starting to open on my right shoulder. I'm screaming in pain, my eyes clamped shut, when suddenly the pressure on my right side is released.

I open my eyes to see that Dotty has flown in and sliced her plasma sword nearly clean through the thick wrist that holds my right arm. The wrist hangs on by a sliver of flesh and tendon, somehow maintaining an iron grip on my right hand. Blood spews from it, covering me in a warm torrent. Cerberus is howling again, dancing in pain and frustration, and I'm shaken like a rag doll in its grip. As my vision steadies, I see in distress that Dotty didn't make it clear after saving me.

She's held now in the bottom set of arms, and Cerberus is preparing to tear her apart. I watch in horror as it holds her between both hands and starts to pull. She's screaming, but no matter how much I squirm I can't get free of the damn thing. Even with its wrist nearly severed, the grip on my right hand is still too strong. *I'm going to watch her die, pulled limb from limb, and I can't do anything to save her. I'm going to watch her die, and then it's going to do the same to me. Fuck fuck fuck.* She's screaming and crying, and all I can do is wait for the end.

Cerberus pauses in pulling her apart, and tries to get something off its back. I stare up to the remaining head, wondering what's happening, until Charon leaps over the back of it. In a great heroic arc he lands right on Cerberus's now up-turned face, and takes a great swipe through the monster's right eye. Blood sprays from the wound as fresh howls pierce the air. Charon leaps again from its face, and races back down its body to the ground below. *Good cat, very very good cat. I owe you all the fish I can find.*

The grip Cerberus has on me loosens slightly, and I'm able to spring my plasma knife and slice through all the fingers that hold me. I fall with the digits in a mess of blood as Cerberus continues to howl. I thrust my wings open and rocket into the air. Every part of me is covered in blood and gore. I level myself with Cerberus's remaining head, and use my wings to rocket forward. I point my right arm knife forwards, with my other hand supporting it. And I hope.

I catch the great beast square in the other eye, and all the energy from my charge sends me up to my shoulder deep in it. Blood and clear fluid from the eye spray over me as I clamp my mouth and eyes shut. My hand reaches Cerberus's remaining brain, and a great shudder goes through its body as my knife digs in. It falls to its knees, and I try to dislodge myself from its eye socket. I jump from the face in time to be smacked by one of the flailing arms. It throws me to the ground in an instant, and when I hit everything goes black.

When I come to, there's a plasma blade pointed at my face. I stare up its length at the holder. She's shaking, crying, but there's resolve in her eyes. I only feel a tenderness for her, and an overwhelming sadness.

"One of us has to die to turn the thing off, that's just the way it is. I don't like this any more than you do. I'm more equipped to lead afterwards than you are, so this only makes logical sense. I'm sorry."

I sit up slowly, and she moves backwards but keeps the blade pointed at me. I might try to fight her, but what's the point? One of us dies, both of us die? And then this was all for nothing? I remember my promise from earlier. *I won't let you die, even if I have to sacrifice myself.* Even with her betrayal, I used her as much as she used me. There's a great resignation in me, but with that a weight slides off my shoulders.

"Dotty, I don't care. I've died so many times already. If one of us has to die to turn the machine off, then fine. It will be me. I know there's going to be massive upheaval after this, someone has to keep it all moving along. That power never interested me. I just want it to end. But if you want to lead, you'll have to settle with the blood on your hands. You can't keep killing people to change things, or this whole place will fall apart."

Her face contracts in anger and defiance at my rebuke. She says nothing, and she doesn't lower the blade. We pause there, her staring down at me in rage, and me looking back at her impassively. Even in her anger, sadness pools in her eyes. *We all die, Dotty, but at least I chose to live well.*

A shadow departs the wall behind her, and I urgently scream, "Charon no, don't hurt her!" He pauses in mid stride, unsure if he wants to listen or tear her apart. "Dotty, put that damn blade down or he will attack you. I'm going willingly now, you don't have to treat me like some prisoner." She looks me in the eyes again, and pulls the shimmering blue blade back in its holster.

I stand then, and we regard each other. I'm so close I could reach out and hold her. I feel the urge to, and see it mirrored in her body language. But the gulf between us is massive. An emotional rift that we can't heal now, and we both know it. There's no more time for us.

Charon walks to my side and glares at Dotty. I reach down to scratch his head affectionately, but he doesn't take his eyes off of her. *It's not just my trust she's broken.* As if waking herself up, Dotty shakes her head and turns around to walk across the room. We follow behind her wordlessly.

There is a small door on each side of the circular room. One must have been how Dotty entered, it's massive enough for Centurions, and on the other side is a smaller, human sized door. It slides open as we approach, and we walk into a stunning antechamber.

The room itself is gleaming, polished silver. It's a half dome that's reflective on every surface. Our images bounce from wall to wall, warped by the curvature of the room. Another similar sized door is on the far wall. The door behind us closes, and we hear it seal shut. The three of us look around in sudden fear as we realize the ease at which we'd been trapped.

Panels part in the seamless walls, and robotic cannons come out to point at us. They're too far away for Dotty to cut them down, and there's too many besides. Dotty flashes me a look, unsure of what to do. Before we can act, there's a loud beep, and the cannons unleash a torrent of high pressure water over us. I squeeze my eyes shut and brace for the impact, but then realize the jets are comforting.

The water washes the gore from our bodies as robotic arms move the cannons to cover every part of us. I open my eyes to see a drain in the floor that swallows the mess, and tension eases from my shoulders as I watch it disappear. The water must have some antiseptic in it. My brutalized hands sting, and then grow pleasantly numb. As I watch, the skin of my hands starts to rapidly rebuild itself. The water stops, the cannons disappear behind their panels. When they close, new openings appear around the circumference of the dome. The room becomes a vortex of warm air as drying fans kick on to all sides of us. In the span of a minute, we are renewed. A chime plays somewhere behind the metal walls, and the door in front of us opens. Behind it we find pure beauty.

This must be the very top of the city. The back wall is transparent glass, and through it is a landscape of rolling hills covered in purple grass. Strange trees. A seemingly endless expanse of land and lush, living things as far as I can see. I rush to the window, and Dotty joins me. We're staring at it, and at each other.

"It's...livable? It's not a wasteland?" I stumble through the words as reality crashes around me. I see the walls of the city for what they are now. They're no longer invisible to me, the boundary where life stops. They're a cage. "Why, how?"

Dotty just shakes her head sadly. "I've no clue, no one has accessed this room in centuries. Even before, only a select few would have seen this. But there's no way to tell if it's livable for us, it could be toxic."

I stand back from the window, shaking in anger, and fear, and disbelief, and then I see it. Next to the window, on the right hand side of the room, is a human shaped enclosure. There's a transparent lid over it. I point to it, and Dotty nods solemnly. The control panel for the Box.

I walk closer, and the lid springs open, inviting me to lay in the body shaped depression. There's a plaque on the exterior surface.

WARNING! Dimensional transit is incredibly dangerous to human life! Side effects may include death, sudden dismemberment, or slight nausea.

It feels like someone's idea of a joke, but I don't get it. Next to the machine is a door. I turn back to Dotty.

"What's through the door?"

She shrugs, disinterested. "Is it open?"

I walk over to it. It's an old, wooden door with an antique brass handle. It looks like some remnant of the long distant past. I try the handle, but it's immovable. The door feels as solid as the walls around it.

I walk back to the machine, resigned now. *There's nothing left to do but climb in.* I stare at it, and think of all the steps it took me to get here. I see my parents continually selling their health to support me. I see Brian helping me create the lie that let me live in the clouds, and then dying to save me from it. I see Micah transforming me into a beautiful monster of a man. I see all the strange and wonderful things I experienced on my journey here. Charon walks up beside me, and when I scratch his ears he presses his big head into my palm.

I look back to Dotty, standing near the glass wall, and find her watching me. Her face is inscrutable, and it makes me feel every inch of the gap between us.

"I don't even know your real name..." She says, her eyes searching mine.

"It's Nick, Nicholas Fiveboroughs. I'm just a Sicko that got a chance to change things, and gambled everything on it. For what it's worth, I'm sorry I lied to you."

She nods at this, her eyes staring at the floor. When she raises her head again, her eyes burn with defiance.

"I know you don't agree with everything I've done, Nick. I've been trying to change things for so long, and it's done nothing. This city's morality is sleeping, and I had to wake it up."

"That's a nice way of talking around the fact that you killed hundreds of people. *Hundreds,* Dotty. Look, if you want absolution, you're not getting it from me. I used to think that any sacrifice was worth it to get what I wanted, and then I realized that was the same justification this city has been using to treat my people like cattle. If you want to break out of a cycle, you can't do it by repeating the same actions."

"They were monsters, Nick, all of them. They're unfit to live in a world that values others."

"And how did killing them go? Half of them probably traded that plague to their drivers and bodyguards, who were kept under a death contract for just wanting to feed their families. All you did was turn on the damn meat grinder, and feed them in. And who are you to make that judgment call of who's a monster? I spent time with those people, and yes they had flaws, but there was humanity in them too."

She laughs angrily at this, and fire lights her eyes.

"Who am I to make that call? Who were you to do the same for the Plague Doctors? Or am I wrong to assume you killed them all? Who were you to take on the guise of a dead man, and use a grieving family's love to ascend? You've been in this world for weeks, but I was born into it. You don't know it like I do. Don't claim some moral high ground just because you find the scale of what I did distasteful."

I wince at the jab, knowing that at least on some of it she's right. The divide between us is only growing. I wanted to mend it, but I'm not sure I can.

We hear a scurrying of metal limbs on the ceiling, like the footfalls of a giant spider, and both our eyes shoot to trace its path. They stop above us, and a rhythmic banging starts.

"Fuck, the Inquisitors are here." Dotty whirls on me, and draws her sword again. Charon crouches and growls throatily at her. "We're out of time, Nick. They'll be through the wall in minutes, and then this was all for nothing. You have to end this thing."

I stare at the sword for a moment, and then bend down and put a calming hand on Charon. He turns to stare into my eyes.

"I'll miss you, boy. Don't hold this against her, she has good intentions."

You are a good man. His voice box hisses quietly, and I scratch him behind the ear. I lean my face in, and kiss the top of his head. Then I rise to look back at Dotty. The pounding in the ceiling has grown louder and syncopated as more Inquisitors join in, so I have to shout to be heard.

"This isn't how I wanted to leave things, Dotty. There's a goodness in you that I fell for, and I don't want you to cheapen it by sacrificing your morals. I wish we had more time together."

She stares at me, the sword lowered now, unsure how to respond. I don't wait for her to. I'm tired of putting this thing off. I've wanted to fix this city for so long, and I won't squander the chance.

I walk back to the machine. The door hisses open as I approach. I walk backwards into the human shaped cavity, and as the door closes over top of me, Dotty rushes forward to say one last thing. I can't hear her though, her mouth moves noiselessly. I shut my eyes. I'm scared for what comes next, but so happy that it finally means the end. The end of suffering for my people, the end of them being used and tossed out. My end.

CHAPTER 18

There's a slow clapping noise as the machine warms up behind me. I clamp my eyes closed. I don't *want* to know how this is going to happen. I just hope it ends suddenly and without pain. I keep them closed, but it starts to sound like the clapping is drawing nearer.

Wait, is it drawing closer?

My eyes spring open. I'm somehow standing in a circular room covered in screens of different sizes. They hang all over, piled on top of each other and threatening to tip over. And more than one has. They're littered on the ground too, face down. There's a man walking towards me, clapping slowly in a mocking appreciation. He's wearing a smart, but nondescript tuxedo and top hat. I recognize his face but can't quite place it.

"Nicholas, wow, I have to say, very well done, boyo! Your epic quest concludes. You achieved your goal, you got the girl—kind of, but we'll call it a win still, you even befriended a cute animal. I mean I just have to say, it's been a hell of a ride."

He claps me on the shoulder, but I don't react. I'm staring at him, my brows furrowing as I recognize him. "You're the old man from the Skyball! I watched glass get dropped on you! You're...dead."

"Oh I always *love* to make a cameo, you know? I laid it on a bit thick though, what did you think of my performance? Convincing? Of course I'm much older than all that really, just a bit of stage reading chap."

"Performance?"

"Oh, my dear boy, there's so much we have to discuss! You wouldn't believe how much anticipation I had, watching you navigate obstacles, sticking it to those damn baddies, and you just kept *almost* dying! Nearly gave an old man an episode!"

"You've been watching?"

He laughs at this, deeply and richly. His whole body arcs backwards in a nearly impossible way, but his top hat stays on.

"Oh boy, the big reveal! Watching? Nick, I've recorded the whole damn thing! We're going to box it up and sell it! Maybe we'll do a book this time, I always love that. And people will read it and they will just EAT YOU UP! Tasty little morsel, lots of heroics, heartbreaking sacrifice, betrayal, some love, some death. Really, I feel a century younger just thinking about it!"

"What the hell is this? Who are you?"

He gives me a smile, somehow broader than any human smile ever could be, and perfect. The distillation of all smiles, ever.

"I'm the Narrator, my boy. I've watched all the different universes, all the different timelines, oh, for forever I guess. It's best not to ask an old man how old he is though, we've all forgotten and secretly just make up a number."

"How did I get here? Am I dead?" I say, starting to look around the room more. There're no signs of Dotty and Charon, of the City. Nothing familiar.

"Oh boy, starting with the deep questions! No, you are in fact very much not dead. Which must feel such a relief. And for how you got here—well let me tell you a little story."

"A long time ago, there was a civilization that was dying out. They lived on this little planet, all bunched in together, but they'd poisoned the thing and made it too hard for them to live on. Very foolish of them, between you and me. And so their *very smart* scientists created giant seed ships, and they loaded a ton of people in them. Like a dying flower, they threw them out into the universe!"

He makes a grand gesture with his arms here, and tiny sparkling things actually shoot out from his hands. As I watch them, the screens around us turn on, and I see it all. Giant tear-dropped shaped ships, screaming through the universe, all propelled in different directions.

"It was a game of averages really. The scientists didn't know how many of their target planets were livable, so they made the ships self-contained. And more than a few of them they miscalculated. They wound up in suns, or shattered in asteroid fields. Some of them are still drifting today."

It plays out on the screens. Some of the ships land on barren, desert planets. Some of them crash into giant balls of fire, and disappear. Some of them touch nothing, just the cold expanse of stars for an eternity. But some of them, and really very few, land on beautiful, lush planets covered in plants of all varieties.

"So the cities were created, all of them separated by an immeasurable distance. Many of them failed, but some survived. And that's where you come in! Centuries later, you were born, and here you are now! What an origin story, right?"

All of this, the city, was designed by someone? They chose this? I feel an anger stirring in me, and focus back on my objective.

"How do I turn off the disease transfer machine?"

He roars in laughter again, his whole body shaking.

"Nick, I love it. I just tell you this grand story of universes and population migration, and you still solely focus on your primary objective. Your *raison d'être*. Okay, I'll give you two options. I can either turn off the Box, as your lot calls it, or I can make it cure all diseases. Which will it be?"

He wiggles his eyebrows at me, but I barely see it. Anger surges through me as my world crashes down.

"It can just *cure* all diseases? It could do that, THIS WHOLE TIME? What is this to you, a fucking game?! There are people dying, every single day! Generations of suffering. And you watched it all?! You're a fucking monster!"

Brian never had to die. My dad never had to die. Fuck this, no one had to ever die from that damn machine.

"Ah my boy, you haven't thought about it deeply enough, I see. Look, how do you keep a self-contained city that creates limited resources and has limited space, from overflowing in population? You see those same *very smart* scientists ran so many simulations, and they all ended in failure. They needed a mechanism, something that would continually limit population growth. That's where the Box comes in. Once they put it in their simulations, everything worked out! They were very excited, but between you and me I don't think they really thought through what living in a society like that would be like. Really if you're faced with the extinction of your entire race, you're willing to make some nasty choices!"

"And so you watch all this, all these different cities suffering, and you're fine with it?"

He sighs, exasperated. "Look here, boyo. There's not much to be done! You're not the first one to ask me to change it. There have been so many. I've seen every permutation of what happens with either decision, and they all end terribly. Choose to turn it off and the population revolts and destroys itself, there's open civil war between the rich and poor. Choose to have it cure all diseases, and the population grows out of control. Food becomes scarce, and then there are revolts, and civil war again."

He shakes his head sadly. "Once someone even decided to have it randomly kill some of the people that used it, now that was a devilishly smart solution. But then it created this strange religious institution around it. That society's still functioning but I would say it might be an even worse way to live. It's a tough choice my boy, but you get to make it! Everything you ever wanted!"

The logic of it swarms my brain. There are outcomes I hadn't seen before. I'm so angry, but also, I just want to give up. *What a waste, this whole life, this whole mission, just a fucking waste.* And then I remember what I saw before I came in here, the flourishing plants outside.

"Wait, and what if the world outside the city *is* livable? Doesn't that give enough room for the population to grow?"

He claps his hands together, excited. "Yes it does! Well, at least for a while. Humans are such a tricky species. You see, you've ruined one planet already, and all the simulations point to the same thing happening again. But for a time, a very long time, you might survive. So is that what you want? To open the city? Do you know for sure that it is livable?"

I came here to turn this thing off for good, but I know what Brian would have wanted here. The elimination of all disease, the elimination of suffering. But if I do that, the population will grow at an unsustainable rate. And if I open the city walls to support them, and the environment isn't livable, then everyone dies. I see the rolling hills of purple plants in my memory, and to my mind they look just like plants I've seen in old photos.

There is no good answer here. This entire time I've been obsessed by the thought of changing this one thing, fixing this one thing, and I never considered the full impact of it. But this way of living, it's not worth it either. If I do nothing, discontent will breed and spread until it makes monsters of us all, and we burn out from the inside. In the end, every option is a gamble then. I might as well gamble to win.

"I want the disease transfer machine to cure all diseases, and I want to open the city."

He leans in close, smiling his impossible smile, and holds his hand up in front of my eyes. Then he snaps his fingers.

"Then it's done! I always love doing that, it makes me feel like a magician. Look, Nick, let's watch it together!"

All the screens change to a giant tear-drop structure sitting in the middle of rolling hills of purple grass. Suddenly, steam hisses all over it, and it segments. One by one, long petal shaped sections uncoil from the tear-drop and expose the city inside. I see the streets that I've lived and breathed, the towers that I've craned my neck to see the top of, all from a new vantage. It opens like a flower seeing the sun for the first time. Some of the screens zoom in to show the wonder of people on the street, the stunned amazement. They're crying, both afraid and enraptured by what they see.

No one dies from an inhospitable environment. No one chokes from poisonous gas or lack of oxygen. They just slowly walk down the arched petals of the city and bask for the first time in real sunlight. And the warmth on their skin feels like warmth on my skin, the tears in their eyes are the same tears in my eyes. I feel so much connection to these people in that moment that I want to caress their faces on the screens. These are my people, finally made whole. Finally given a chance. I've ached for this moment for so long, and never knew it.

I dreamed to shut down the Box, if even just long enough to break the cycle, but this is what I really wanted. No more chains to their money, to their food, to their damn city. We can struggle and thrive, not confined by the roles our birth set for us. How silly all those towers seem now, in the vast expanse of a world that is open, lush, and alive. *Freedom*. I can taste the word on my tongue, but I won't speak it. I won't break the spell of transformation that I'm watching.

The Narrator breaks it for me when he claps me on the shoulder again. "Now, now, boyo. It's not all fun and games, look at this!" The screens zoom in, all the way to the top of the city, to the room where Dotty and Charon are. The room where I am. Inquisitors swarm the walls surrounding the room, tearing at the structure to get in. "It looks like you've made something very, very angry. Those things are one of the city's defense mechanisms, did you know that? In most cities they don't have this response to meeting with me, so maybe it was the destruction at the Skyball, or killing all the Centurions, or taking out that big beast outside. It's tough to say, but I really don't think you'll make it out of this one. Sorry chap, you did well though! Take heart that you probably made a difference."

I stare at the scene, watching them tear into the structure. They dig in, ripping their hands apart, grinding their arms off, until they're only left to smash their heads against the wall, and die in a heap. With each broken thing that falls, another immediately replaces it. They're zealous, undeterred by their own destruction. They're like a singular wave of metal smashing into the walls, and even as the wave breaks apart, the structure weakens. It's horrifying to watch. For the first time, I know with a certainty that I'll die. That when they breach through that wall, Dotty, Charon, and I will disappear so totally under the crush of them that we may never be found.

There always had to be a price.

The man holds up his hand, as if a thought just struck him. "You know what?! It would be fun if I gave you a way out! Secret access to the world between worlds, and the vision to see the map. I'm seeing it now, sequel potential! Another adventure, more drama, more excitement. And the highest stakes you can imagine—Oh, I can practically taste the tension already!"

He claps his hands together excitedly, and then grabs my hand and shakes it vigorously. There's a burning, searing pain in my palm, and I yank it back from his grasp. Outlined against my healing palm is new skin in the shape of a key.

"Great to meet you face to face, Nick. I usually get so bashful in front of actors, you know it really is impressive what you lot do. I'm your biggest fan, I'd say! Well carry on then, chap. Good luck and all that. We'll meet again some day!"

The room of screens fades, and the Narrator disappears, like they were never there at all. Like they were some dream. And then reality comes swooping back in. I'm stuck in a human shaped cavity with a transparent covering, in a room that's being swarmed by mechanical things that want to tear me and my friends apart.

The machine springs open, Dotty stands on the other side. She's wide eyed in terror, staring at me.

"Nick, you're alive? The city, it just opened up. What the hell happened in there?"

The whole room echoes with the din of metallic clawing on the outer surface. An Inquisitor's spiked hand breaks through the ceiling, and the noise grows much louder.

"I don't think we have time to talk, Dotty, it looks like we're about to have a lot of company! We need to get out of here!"

She shrugs, resigned, as she turns to look at the hands that reach in to widen the hole. "And go where, Nick? The city wants to destroy us for the intrusion. Even if we get out of here you know they'll keep hunting us. And there's no way out of this room anyways, you already tried that door." She motions to the wooden door behind the machine.

I remember the key imprint in my hand, and when I look down I see it's still there. It's a faint outline, like a new crease in the skin of my palm.

"No time to explain, I have a key now!" I rush to the door, and her and Charon follow me. When I grab the handle there's a great unlatching inside the door. It swings open under the lightest pressure. The three of us gape at what we see.

What should be behind this door is an exit from the city, spatially that's the only thing that makes sense. We should see the rolling grasses and trees visible out the window. We should be discussing how we'd get down from this height without dying. There is none of that.

Instead, there is the endless black expanse of space in front of us. Stars and galaxies swirl around and light the room. It seems to stretch out forever, and the infinity of it captivates us. I hear a noise from behind that breaks the reverie, and the three of us swirl around in time to see the first Inquisitors land in the room.

"TIME TO GO!" I scream, and we launch ourselves through the door. It clicks softly shut behind us. Then there is total silence.

I look around, and the door we came through is just one of many. Doors stand in a surrealist landscape all around us, and behind them are more doors. They stretch all the way to the horizon, in every direction. There's nothing behind any of them, just frames standing on their own. I stand up, but nearly fall back down when I see what we're standing on. Beneath our feet are an endless array of galaxies, suns, stars, planets. *The Cosmos.*

Then I see the ghost lines. Mostly transparent shapes stretch in front of each of us like a strangely curving path, and when I turn back to the door, I see they extend behind us as well. They're hard to see, but a slight distortion from light warping at their edges makes them visible from certain angles. In their shape are all the positions my body took as I entered the room, and next to it is a trail left by Dotty and Charon. As Dotty stands, she expands to fill the shape in front of her. The path didn't change as she moved, but was in exactly the correct position. *Like it knew exactly where she'd move.* I continue to follow her path into the distance, and see that it moves at an angle from my own.

"What is this place?!" Dotty says, breaking me from my thoughts.

"I have no idea."

"How did you know we could get in here? Nick, what the fuck is going on?"

So we sit down, in the middle of swirling galaxies, and I explain it all to her. I explain about meeting the Narrator, what he said, and the choices he gave. I tell her about the key, and how I knew it was for the door. I tell her about books, and sequels, and all the other strange things he said. And then we're both quiet for a long, long time. Charon rests besides me, his head on my lap. I scratch behind his ears and try to ignore the pressing potential of the paths in front of us. And the knowledge that they head in separate directions.

There's a peacefulness in this place that we all needed, something wholesome and fulfilling about just existing here together. About not being chased, not being almost killed, not struggling for once to achieve some distant goal. We're all alive, together. There's an urge inside me to just let the past go.

"So then, what's next?" Dotty asks.

I shrug. "We can't go back, I'd bet those Inquisitors have a very long memory. We might not be able to ever go back." I glance towards our paths again. *Can Dotty see them? She hasn't said anything yet.* Something the Narrator said rings in my head, *Secret access to the world between worlds, and the vision to see the map.*

The reality of being forced from our home, the only thing we've ever known, rests on both of us. I see it in her face just like I feel it in mine. I'll never see my mother again, never know if Josephine is okay, never share another laugh with Micah. The streets I grew up with and know like my own hands. All of it's gone.

Dotty sighs deeply, staring off into the cosmos. "Okay, so we're stuck here then. We can't go back. I guess this is what the Narrator intended. There's nothing to do now but explore some of these other doors. I'm glad you didn't die in that machine, Nick."

Anger surges in me suddenly. "You're glad I didn't die? In the machine you pushed me into *at sword point*, the one you thought *would kill me*?" I scoff. "Tell that to the hundreds of people you helped poison. Tell that to Brian. Or are you glad they died? I've done horrible things too, Dotty, but at least I'm trying to atone."

Dotty stands, her face roiling with flashes of anger at each thing I say. "You're so damn self-righteous, I can't stand it! There's blood on my hands, trust me I know that. But with the Box changed, and the politicals cowed, the city can actually grow. We gave them an opportunity. It can finally move forward, Nick, and I don't regret that," she pauses, and then as if speaking more to herself, quietly says, "There wasn't another way."

"How do you know that? We just transformed the fundamental way the city works. We removed the leadership. We created a power vacuum, and that's an opportunity for more than just positive change. I just hope the better parts of our nature wins." With every word, the rift between us is growing. Our anger is building it into a chasm, and as much as I need to say these things, they feel like a knife in my gut when I do. *I just want her to apologize. I'm so tired. I just want things to be like they were.*

"I'm not doing this. You won't make me feel ashamed." Dotty reaches down and grabs her plasma sword off the ground. For a brief moment, I'm afraid that she's going to use it on me. She notices the flash of fear in my eyes, and I see the pain it causes her. "Goodbye, Nick, I don't know where the hell we are or where we're heading, but I'm doing it on my own."

I want to stop her, tell her to stay, tell her we can forgive each other. But for once, the words stick in my mouth. They feel uncertain, unready to be said. I look into the far distance, and between the doors that dot the landscape, I wonder if I can see our paths joining again. I turn back to her, and give a nod. "Please stay safe, Dotty. I hope I see you again."

She says nothing, but nods in response. I watch as she turns around, and follows the path that I saw when we entered this place. The one that leads away from me. The one that I knew she'd take as soon as I saw it. Eventually, she disappears behind doors that obscure my view, and only then do I sit back down. Charon slumps against me, and I lay down in the safety of the stars and swirling galaxies. In darkness, I rest.

Ian Patterson is many things. Importantly here, he's the author of Transference, Book One of the Narrator Cycle. He's also an engineer, cyclist, foodie, coffee lover, cat dad, human father, and reader of books. Preferably, thick books that deal with strange things and big ideas. He's dreamed of being an author for decades, but finally began the journey with the birth of his first daughter. This is an objectively terrible time to start work that requires quiet concentration, and he knows it, but he loves the chaos nonetheless. He lives in Colorado with his wonderful family.

Newsletter / Fiction Blog:
https://ipatterson.substack.com